THE LEGEND OF THE SWAN

Witness Tree 1

Beverly Sims

MENAGE AMOUR

Siren Publishing, Inc.
www.SirenPublishing.com

A SIREN PUBLISHING BOOK
IMPRINT: Ménage Amour

THE LEGEND OF SUMMER SWAN
Copyright © 2009 by Beverly Sims

ISBN-10: 1-60601-517-6
ISBN-13: 978-1-60601-517-9

First Printing: June 2009

Cover design by Jinger Heaston
All cover art and logo copyright © 2009 by Siren Publishing, Inc.

Printed in the U.S.A.

PUBLISHER
Siren Publishing, Inc.
www.SirenPublishing.com

DEDICATION

To the wonderful American Indians who were our forefathers and mothers and whose lives gave birth to our great Nation.

THE LEGEND OF SUMMER SWAN

Witness Tree 1

BEVERLY SIMS
Copyright © 2009

Prologue

I have been standing here for 200 years. I have reached the end of my time on this prairie, but oh, the things I have seen. Now the cancer of rot inside my trunk will win out over the life I have provided for creatures large and small on my branches and in my roots. Such is the nature of nature. It has been a good life and I will share some tales of truth as I saw them.

I grew as a sapling beside my mother oak where her trunk and leaves sheltered me through the heat of the sun and the cold of the winters when all things hibernated. My first memories are from the year she died. It was the time of buffalo and Indians. Millions of brown and black bison roamed the plains freely. And where the buffalo roamed, so did the Indians hunt them.

In years to come, this time and the people who lived here will be forgotten. Most of what I have seen is of little importance, but the happenings in one village need to be told and remembered forever. Here I tell "The Legend of Summer Swan."

Chapter 1

The hunters stood on a hill and watched the endless ocean of slow moving characters as they grazed in the valley below. The chief, Soaring Eagle, seldom hunted anymore. He was wise and knew at his age he would be a deterrent rather than an asset to the band, but his old eyes were still keen as he noted a few aged, crippled, or young ones that had wandered away from the buffalo herd.

He pointed them out to the hunters. From his vantage point, he could see the men as they moved quietly down the hill, with his two sons out in front. He sighed and for a moment remembered the day that they were born.

* * * *

It was the third time She Who Smiles had grown large with child. The first two were girls. He named the first, Brown Fawn because her eyes were large and doe-like as a speckled fawn. The second was Crazy Eyes for her crossed eyes. He loved his daughters, but secretly yearned for a son, a strong son to lead the tribe when his time passed.

She Who Smiles woke him one cold, windy morning. "It is time, my husband. I will leave you and find a sheltered place to drop my burden."

"No, I will help you."

"It is wrong for you to see the ugliness of birth. It is for the mother only to witness. But you may help me with warm blankets and moccasins. Oh, yes, and a shawl. No skirt or pants. It must be clear for my ease in squatting. I must hurry, as it is near."

Soaring Eagle did as she asked, but did not let her go by herself. He helped her onto his horse and together they rode to the place she had picked earlier. It was in a grove of oaks with a huge dying tree and a sapling that gave some shelter.

She slid off the horse and spread one of the blankets on the ground between her legs and the other over her shoulders. "Now, go, Husband. I will return soon."

I watched her. Even a young tree somehow knows that in her pain, she was losing strength. Finally, she dropped to her knees and pressed her back against my mother's trunk. She cried and screamed for what to my young mind seemed like forever. As suddenly as it had started, it stopped. Her screams no long rent the quiet of the prairie.

Soaring Eagle fed his daughters and watched the sun climb in the sky. Something was wrong. He knew it. She should have been back by now. Unable to bear waiting any longer, he jumped on his horse and raced to the birthing place. He saw her form on the ground. Blood stained the blankets. Between her legs, he saw a small head, but She Who Smiled did not move. He picked her up and climbed his horse with her in his arms. He felt her breath on his cheek and knew she was still alive.

The people heard his shouts as he raced among the tents to where the medicine man, Hook Nose lived. The old man, wearing various animal bones around his neck, stepped out of his buffalo skin tepee. "What is all this shouting about, Soaring Eagle?"

"Cannot you see? My wife is dying. The baby has not come out. You must help me."

He slid off his horse and ran for the tent opening. Hook Nose stood in his way. It is the way of the gods. This child in not meant to walk this earth."

"My wife, save my wife ..."

Again, the old man shook his head. "If she dies, it is also the will of the gods. There is nothing I can do unless you want me to give her something to make her end quicker and less painful." With that, he reentered his home, dropping the canvas behind him.

As gently, as he could he laid her down upon their robe-covered bed in their tepee. She moaned softly. He rubbed her lips with water from the cooking bowl by the fire circle. She responded with another moan, and then let out a scream as the child burst out between her legs.

Soaring Eagle was unaware of the woman who entered so quietly behind him and now knelt beside him. White Rabbit was one of his father's wives. She quickly bit the cord tying the child to its mother. She held the baby up by its feet and slapped the tiny buttocks. A strong cry rent the air and those all listening outside heard and smiled. White Rabbit grinned at Soaring Eagle and pointed to the tiny penis. He returned her smile and lowered his head to his wife's face. "We have a son, wife. He is strong. You have done good."

She did not reply, but screamed again. White Rabbit placed the infant in his arms and resumed her position between the woman's legs. "The gods are cruel, Soaring Eagle. They have sent another. It is bad luck and both must de destroyed or evil will visit the tribe." Again, she bit the cord, slapped its bottom, and turned to expose another tiny penis.

Soaring Eagle had two sons. In his heart, he knew he would never let anyone touch either of them. He leaned over She Who Smiles, who was so weak she could barely shake her head. Another scream, then silence. He felt her lips and found no breath. He knew she died giving him his sons, and he vowed to her that her death was not for nothing. He bowed his head and cried for the woman he loved.

White Rabbit spoke, "Soaring Eagle, there is a third child. It is a girl, but died with She Who Smiles. This is a terrible sign." She laid the two babies beside their mother and covered them with a buffalo skin blanket before she left to gather other women for the preparation of the body for burial.

Soaring Eagle lay with his wife in his arms, her head on his shoulder, as they had snuggled so many nights after their passion waned. Never again would she cry out under him. Never again would he suckle her breasts and taste the milk meant for the babies. Never again anything. He cried.

* * * *

The commotion outside his tepee woke him. Both his sons were awake. For the first time, he thought about how he would feed them, but those thoughts were fleeting as the Hook Nose pushed into Soaring Eagle's abode.

"Give me the babes. Sacrificing them to the gods will appease their displeasure. More than one child at a time will bring a generation of misfortune to our tribe."

Soaring Eagle jumped to his feet and blocked the smelly old man. "You will not touch my sons. They are mine and I will protect them from even you, old man. The gods took She Who Smiles, but they will not have my children."

Hook Nose shoved Soaring Eagle, knocking him to the side. He bent over the bloody robe on the bed, but before he could take a child, Soaring Eagle pulled his knife, grabbing the man by the neck. With one quick slide, the head hung only by the skin on the backside. He dropped the dead man to the floor, the blood pumped out and covered the babes in red. Soaring Eagle feared the red blood was a sign, but he had no idea what kind of a sign it was.

Holding both sons in one arm, Soaring Eagle pushed outside. He held the blood-dripping knife in his other hand and spoke softly, "No man will harm my sons. These two male children will grow to adulthood, as do sons of other chief and chief's sons. Anyone who challenges will die at my hand. Does anyone object?"

Chapter 2

White Rabbit met Soaring Eagle outside his father's tepee and motioned him inside. His father, Cold Wind, sat on a buffalo robe placed on the dirt floor, watching the fire. He nodded Soaring Eagle forward and indicated he should lay the infants beside him on the robe. He carefully slid aside the robes covering each and examined him. Finally, he covered the babes and nodded to his son.

"What has happened is destined to bring the gods' disfavor upon the land. How do you answer for this, my son?"

"Father, my sons are strong and alert. They will grow straight and just beside me as I grew by you. With wisdom, they will learn the ways of our world and we will prosper, which will please the gods. Our arrows will be truer, our horses faster, our wives more fertile, our hunts more successful, and our enemies more easily defeated."

Cold Wind listened and sat without speaking for several minutes. "How do you intend to raise them without a wife? Who will feed them? Who will make their robes? Have you thought of these things? Or of your daughters?"

Soaring Eagle hung his head before lifting it to look directly into his father's eyes. "Yes, father, I have. I will find some women to suckle them and slaves to care for them and their needs. May I ask White Rabbit to help me?"

His father nodded. "Leave the little ones here with her. Go to Brave Hawk and ask if his new slave can help until you return with your own. Her girl child died yesterday and she has milk to nourish your sons. Now, go and let me ponder your punishment for killing Hook Nose."

"But, Father he tried …"

"No more! The man was doing as the gods' decree. You were wrong and you must pay for his death. The council will decide what is to be done or even if the little ones are to live. Do not say another word. Go and be gone from my sight."

* * * *

Soaring Eagle left as soon as he talked to Brave Hawk who was reluctant to let his slave nurture the babes. He finally agreed, but only until Soaring Eagle found another wet woman.

Soaring Eagle sensed hostility everywhere so he left immediately. To remain would bring wrath on him and his sons. No one offered to ride with him in his search. No one wanted to risk angering the council by helping him.

He took only his horse, his weapons, a small bag of dried meat and his sleeping robe. He meant to find a camp to either buy or steal any wet woman he found for his sons. He knew their friends would not give him nor sell to him any of their women, but perhaps they had a slave or two they would part with.

The two camps he visited the next three days were understanding about his lost wife, but could not help him. He skirted another camp, which he knew he would meet his death if he entered. Frustrated, he turned toward home taking a different route.

Suddenly his luck changed. Under a copse of juniper, he saw a woman squatting to give birth. He watched as the child dropped to the ground. She lifted it and bit the cord that tied them together. She held it by the ankles and swatted its tiny bottom, but no cry came. She repeated the slap but again to no avail. She turned the child so that her mouth covered its tiny nose and mouth. She took deep breaths from the tiny body and then released air back into it.

Even from his distance away from her, he was sure the child would never take that first breath. He knew without seeing it up close, because the woman was crying. She slowly wrapped her child in a small buffalo skin that was to be its swathing blanket. She cleaned herself with leaves and small scraps of skins. She sat down, away from the signs of birthing, with her back against the large dying tree. It seemed fit to her that she and her dead child would wait out the rest of their lives under such a tree.

Her head was bowed, her legs pulled up to her chest, and the child in her arms. She did not see the two painted men on foot came around the strand of trees, one from each direction. One grabbed her, shoving a large rock into her mouth to gag her and held her while the other tied her. The second one left and returned with three horses. They lifted her up onto a horse and tried to pull the bundle from her arms. She kicked out with the feet and hit at them with the arm not holding the child. It became apparent even to the men that the child was dead. They spoke to one another. One shrugged and took the reins of the woman's horse and led it to his horse, where he tied it to follow behind him.

Soaring Eagle felt sorrow for the woman and her pain. He knew the woman would die harder than her child had. It was best there was no child now, because a wet woman has only so much milk, perhaps not enough for the twins and another one.

He had no idea where these two were from, only that they were not from a tribe on his plains. He followed them at a safe distance and stayed in the dark close by when they camped. He watched them drink from the container. He assumed by their actions that it was something that made them drunk. All he had to do was wait.

They passed the container back and forth until the first one, then the second, dropped to the ground. Superstition kept them away from the woman, as it was bad luck in most tribes to join with a bleeding female. Soaring Eagle noted that she sat away from the fire, trembling from the cold as her robe had fallen away. With her hands tied behind her back, he knew she could not reach it to pull it back. It seemed to matter little to her. Perhaps, she grieved her dead child beside her and prayed the cold night would take her life, he thought.

Soaring Eagle waited until her head dropped to her chest and her eyes closed. Without making sound, he walked calmly into the sparse camp, bent over the first prone man then the other, and slit both throats. He picked up the robe from the ground and wrapped it around the freezing woman. He dug the rock from her mouth and dribbled water between her lips from his water bag. She cried out in fear as he picked her up to settle her, still tied, on her horse.

He handed her the remains of her baby while he dug a shallow grave for it. He had no tools but his knife and tomahawk with which to open the earth, but under the trees, the ground was soft from years of leaves and needles. She watched him carefully and slowly held out her arms for him to take her bundle. He nodded and carefully placed the tiny form in the ground and covered it. He wrestled a large rock until it lay atop the grave so that nothing could disturb the eternal slumber of the babe.

He gathered the weapons and horses. He mounted his horse and headed toward home. He had no idea what he would find there, but he never dreamed of such horrors.

Chapter 3

What he found was fire and death.

As he neared his camp, smoke filled the sky over the horizon. He urged his horse into a dead run, slowing only as he reached the rise above the encampment. He dismounted and ran forward where he flopped to the ground on his stomach to conceal himself as he looked below.

There was no longer any need to conceal himself, the enemy was gone, taking with them heart and soul of the village. At first, he could not comprehend the carnage. His stomach turned and his eyes filled with unshed tears.

He led the horses as he walked down the hill. The woman behind him was crying softly as she saw the destruction, the destruction that caused his blood to boil and his heart to break. His father's tepee was a burnt skeleton with Cold Wind's bleeding, scalp less body in the dust in front. The body had several arrows protruding, leaving no doubt he had fought bravely.

Pink Flower, Soaring Eagle's mother, was the first wife. Her body now hung, naked from a tree branch. It appeared that she and other elderly women had been targets of much torture before they died.

He found White Rabbit on the ground, similarly tortured with the addition of rape, probably many times from the looks of her corpse. Bile filled his throat as he wandered what was left of the village.

Soon it became apparent that the younger men were gone. They would never leave the village unprotected in the event of a raid, so this was obviously a surprise. Hunting? Yes, he was sure that is where they were. His peaceful people had fought the invaders, but without the younger warriors, they were doomed from the start.

The few men left in the village were mostly older ones who managed to kill a few enemies before they were cut to pieces. He rolled over enemy bodies looking for signs of their identity, but the clues told him nothing, nothing except that they were not from his world. From the south, undoubtedly renegades. He suspected them to be from the same people who had captured the woman who stood behind the horse, still tied.

He returned to her horse, lifted her down, and cut her rawhide bindings. She moved away from him, turned her back, and squatted to relieve herself. A puddle of blood reddened the ground beneath her. Soaring Eagle found a piece of animal skin on the ground and tossed it in front of her, before he strode off, leaving her to her woman thing alone.

He found his sweet daughters dead, one from an arrow, the other from a knife. There was no sign of his sons. The attackers had taken the small boys and young women with them. His pain was unbelievable as he held his little girls in his arms. His sons were safe as captives, at least for the time being.

Looking around, he determined that there had been at least to dozen enemies, minus the by five killed by his people. The horses were gone and their store of dried meat and robes were missing. Anything of value was stolen or burnt.

* * * *

Summer Swan watched him and understood his pain without knowing the circumstances. She knew only that the dead girls were his daughters from the way he picked them up and held them to his chest. She grieved for her own daughter, who never drew a breath, but her heart was large and she grieved for all the lost souls and the men they left behind.

She saw him hold the old man's body in his arms, rocking back and forth, as he raised his eyes to the sky. He cut down the dangling corpses and laid one next to the man he mourned over, crying openly. Perhaps the pair was his parents. Her loss seemed small compared to his. Two daughters and both parents was more than she could imagine. How many of the others were his family, she wondered. No doubt, they were all his friends. She remembered the loss of her mother and tried to imagine the pain over one lost person multiplied by four, but she could not.

She said nothing as he walked through the smoking remains of his home, as if unable to accept what he saw. Finally, he began to repack their horses. In the distance, she heard the beat of horses' hooves. The returning hunters probably had seen the smoke, too, and were ready for a fight. Their weapons were at ready, but they slowed their race into the village as they took in the carnage.

* * * *

Little Bear was the first to arrive. He jumped from his horse, knife out as he ran toward Soaring Eagle. His intention was apparent even to Soaring Eagle who saw the fury in his eyes. He meant to kill Soaring Eagle, who stepped aside just in time, grabbing the attacker around the neck. He pulled Little Bear's hand with the knife up to the warrior's throat.

"Stop, Little Bear. Why are you trying to kill me? We are friends, comrades."

"No longer. You are the reason for this, for the loss of our families and our village. You murdered the shaman and brought evil to us when you refused to destroy the fruit of your loins when your wife gave birth to more than one child. So, kill me if you like because I will kill you if you do not."

"Will killing me bring back your family or your homes? A band of heathens from the south did this, from the look of their paint and clothes. Our friends would protect us, not slaughter us. The gods did not do it either. Men did and those we must find and take revenge. They have taken the young women and small boys for slaves and their pleasures. They have murdered our fathers and mothers, grandfathers and grandmothers, our wives and older sons. Instead of attacking me, you should be riding beside me in your search for what is ours, in search of our kidnapped people and to kill the marauders."

There were murmurs of agreement and mumbles of discontent. Finally, Man of Horses, Soaring Eagle's uncle and brother of the dead chief Cold Wind, spoke. "He is right. We will follow and destroy them, but first we must tend our dead." He pointed to three young warriors who had no wives or children. "You travel to our friendly neighbors and tell them what has happened." The three ran to their horses and sped off at a full run.

Someone finally noticed the young woman standing away from them and pointed to her. "Soaring Eagle, who is this woman?"

Soaring Eagle looked at her as if she was something he had never seen before, and then remembered where she came from. He motioned to her to come forward, which she did with her head bowed. "What is your name, woman? Who is your husband?"

"I am called Summer Swan because my neck is so long. My husband was killed by a raging buffalo in a hunt last time the leaves changed color."

"I am sorry for your loss, of your husband and your child. I took you instead of returning you to your people because I needed a wet woman to suckle my sons. Take your horse and go back to your village."

"Wait. Please. Let me stay with you. When you find your sons, you will need me then." She bowed her head again. "I was a slave to my husband who took me as a wife. The first wives hate me. Without him for protection, I will not live long. They did not kill me before because I was heavy with child and the tribe looked out for me. Now there is no child and no need to keep me alive. For me to return will mean death." She lifted her head and looked directly into his eyes. "Please, let me go with you, for your sons' sake."

Tall Tree stepped forward. "She will slow us down. She can stay here until we return."

Soaring Eagle looked around. "What will shelter her? What will feed her as there is nothing left? We will take her with us. And she is right, she will be help when we get our children back."

"Then, Soaring Eagle, she is your responsibility. If she lags, you will have to deal with it because we will not stop or slow for her." Tall Tree addressed Soaring Eagle, but looked at Summer Swan. "Do you understand?" She nodded and dropped her head again. Without a word, she moved to the first body she found, a child, and picked it up as the men built burial platforms.

Chapter 4

I watched them from beneath my mother's dying limbs. I did not see what they saw after they left me, but I heard the tale many times over the years. This is what the elders told the young ones over and again.

After the burials of the bodies, the warriors and Summer Swan rode their mounts with water skins and fresh buffalo tied meat behind them and on their packhorses. Soaring Eagle tied each of the horses from the men he killed to one of the packhorses. They would be necessary to bring home the ones who were missing. He looked up at the sky where vultures circled the camp thanked his namesakes for their support and the pictures of his sons he saw in the sky with them.

The marauders were easy to follow. It was as if their confidence won out over common sense, as if they had no concern about anyone following them. The attitude angered the warriors. The second thing Soaring Eagle noted was that they were traveling a slow pace, again conveying their confidence. He urged his band to ride hard until the horses tired. They camped that evening by a small creek but did not build fires to cook their food. The only thing they had that night was some rawhide strips their enemies had missed in the village.

* * * *

Now at the fireless campsite, Summer Swan climbed a slight rise and found a tree where she could relieve herself and clean her body again. As she started back down, she heard talking and screams carried to her by the wind from some distance away. She ran down the hill to the first man she saw and told him her news. He announced it to all, and she watched as they returned to the crest where she had been. When they returned, they sent two young warriors, two that had joined them after spreading the word to the neighboring villages, to spy on the enemy camp. The pair of young braves returned at a full gallop. Summer Swan took their horses to the creek for water, but listened to the report. One of the scouts spoke breathlessly, tired from the hard ride, "They are raping our women, even the young girls. I saw no boys or babies, just the naked women. Ours are the only females in camp and they will surely be dead by morning if we don't stop them."

Tall Tree spoke, "My wife and daughter are there, as are some of your families. We must attack them now. We will take our horses as close as we dare. Did you see guards posted?" The young men looked at the ground. "Apparently, you two did not to your job as expected. Woman, you will remain here and tend the horses. We will return for you when you are needed." She nodded. Summer Swan watched the men, as they leaped onto their horses and moved as quietly as deer through the brush and tall grass. Summer Swan followed at a distance, but close enough to see what was happening. When the warriors neared the camp, on foot they moved closer. Their captive women were fighting the assaults as best they could, much to the pleasure of their captors. Tall Tree's young wife, Dewdrops, was on her back while a fat man with a large belly squatted between her legs, moving in and out of her. He held her arms above her head with one meaty hand while he squeezed her breasts with the other and laughed as she fought him.

* * * *

It was more than Tall Tree could take. This young woman he married only to protect her from randy young warriors and he planned to keep her pure until she was old enough to be a real wife. They wed on her 14th year and Little Crane came two years later. Dewdrops never did enjoy their mating, so he seldom approached her. Nevertheless, in many ways, he did love her and seeing her as she suffered turned him into a devil.

He jumped upright from his crawling position, and ran into the camp, hunting ax raised. His throw was perfect, as the fat man collapsed on the prone woman. The rest of his men followed. There was not much of a fight, as the enemy was unprepared and many had too much to drink. When the confrontation ended, not all the enemy had died. Two wounded men they did not kill, so they could answer questions. In the end, they begged for death.

Tall Tree rolled the man off his wife and knelt beside her. She was dead and he was glad, in a way. Now she would suffer no more. Her life had not been a happy one. Even the child gave her no pleasure, and she was quite willing to let him raise the child.

Within seconds, he began to run from tepee to tepee calling out the name of his precious daughter. When she did not answer, he knew she was gone, too. He dropped to his knees, head down and allowed his tears to fall. He felt a hand on his shoulder and looked up to see the sad face of the woman Summer Swan. She dropped to the ground beside him and pressed his head to her chest, offering him comfort he so sorely needed.

Chapter 5

Soaring Eagle found his sons, alive and well, with one of his nieces who fed them with sugar water in a rag. Her name was Little Crane for her long legs. She was five years old, even a bit too young for the carnal urges of the men who stole her. Soaring Eagle hugged her close as he knelt beside her. She cried huge tears and hiccupped loudly until they both laughed. "I am proud of you, Little Crane. How did you know to feed the babies?"

"I watched my mamma nurse puppies when their mother died under the buffalo feet after she followed my father on a hunt. I got to keep one. Her name was Lucky, but she sure was not lucky, was she? Mamma said the puppies would die if we did not feed them, so she taught me what to do. We fed the puppies milk, but I did not have any, so water was all I could give the babies." Her face clouded. "I think Mamma is dead because she stopped moving after … after … after."

Soaring Eagle turned to where she pointed through the open flap, it was his sister, his favorite sister Dewdrops, Tall Tree's wife. He saw the woman called Summer Swan comforting the man, as did Little Crane at the same moment. She ran to him, nearly knocking him over as she rushed into his arms. He kissed her tears away and turned them both so that the child could not see her mother's face and torn body.

Soaring Eagle thought Tall Tree seemed to calm, but only a bit, as he lifted his daughter in his arms. They were close friends, more so than some brothers. Soaring Eagle knew the girl child was all he had left in the world after his son died at the village. He had been a strapping boy who begged to hunt this time with his father, who refused his request, telling him he must stay behind to protect the village. Weeks later Tall Tree told Soaring Eagle that he felt bile in his throat as he remembered the boy's disappointed face as he turned away. As long as he lived, that would be the face Tall Tree recalled when he thought of his boy-child, and Soaring Eagle understood. Soaring Eagle saw the woman rise from the ground by Tall Tree, looking in his direction. Within seconds, she was at his side taking one child in each arm. "You must help me," Summer Swan said. "Pull my shirt up so the babes can find my breasts. After this first time, I shall feed them one at a time, but they are starving and I am hurting with the fullness of milk."

She Who Smiles was the only woman he had ever touched until now. He hesitated, not wanting to be even this close to a woman other than his beloved, but he did as instructed, careful not to touch her skin. But, he could not take his eyes off his sons, even as she turned away for privacy from men's eyes. Each child sucked and butted her tit as small pigs on their mother.

Seldom had She Who Smiles let him watch as she nourished their daughters, but he did not think they were as strong and demanding as the two boys seemed to be. For an instant, he recalled that there had been a third child, but forced that memory away. All that mattered now was his sons, drinking from the huge breasts of his own captive who had given her up freedom to feed his children.

Soaring Eagle forced himself to look away. All around men bowed over dead wives and daughters or standing with arms around those who had survived. There was carnage everywhere. Two of the younger women were still living as they hung from tree limbs, moaning and dying.

* * * *

One of them was Tall Tree's younger wife who barely more than a girl. She was his wife in name only because he felt no desire to consummate his marriage to a child. He married her only to protect her as he had promised the mother of the child on her deathbed. He saw her pain and carefully took her into his arms. He kissed her face one last time before quickly slitting her throat. He could allow her an easy death as her's would have been long and painful. Somehow that made it easier for him, but not from his little daughter. She had now lost her mamma and her friend. He picked up his wife's body and moved it to lie beside Dewdrops. He took Little Crane in his lap again as he sat on the ground by his two wives and he and the child grieved together.

The warriors cut several trees to make platforms for their dead. Instead of one for each, they laid the bodies as close together as possible and the chant that would take their souls to their gods. The attackers lay where they fell, food for vultures and scavengers. Tall Tree looked backward from his horse where his daughter rode in front of him. "Being food for carrion is better than they deserve. Now, let us go home."

Chapter 6

They rode toward where home had been, each adult with his or her own thoughts. By count, Summer Swan found there were nine living children, including the twins and Little Crane. The six others were all smaller than she was, but all were big enough to walk short distances, but for the twins who had to be carried. There were four females, three of whom might not even make the trip back. She and Soaring Eagle each carried one of the twins, still unnamed. Little Crane told her that in their tribe the grandfather always named the male children, but Soaring Eagle would ask the eldest warrior, his uncle, to do so when they resettled.

They stopped early beside a small creek, allowing them all the luxury of bathing downstream from where they drew their water. The children splashed and played with the wonderful innocence of children, forgetting momentarily what had happened. Summer Swan thought how fortunately the children were to be able to put the horror out of their minds, if only for a few minutes.

Summer Swan brought water to heat by the fire, and then carefully bathed the ailing women. She washed the bruised faces and open wounds before trying to give relief to the soreness and rips between their legs. They all three were spared rape because it was their moon cycle, but that did not stop the savages from torturing them. After the babes ate, Summer Swan laid them on a buffalo skin and asked Soaring Eagle for a knife. He looked at her questioningly, but handed her one from his rope belt.

They had no tents to erect but they had nearly fresh buffalo meat for substantial meals. They expected Summer Swan to do the cooking, but she was walking away from camp, out onto the prairie. They watched her for several minutes before realizing she was seeking plants and roots that she gathered and carried in her rolled up skirt. She returned with things that the white people would later call catnip, aloe, coneflower, and juniper. These she crushed or boiled and when they were cool, she returned to the injured women. She spread the mashed plants on the bites and open wounds carefully but even then, they cried out in pain. The boiled catnip leaves she put to their lips, trying to get them to drink as it would calm them and make them sleepy, and their pain would subside. She used the sticky liquid from the aloe on the burned spots.

One of the twins whimpered, immediately followed by the other. She returned to them, put one to her tit, and patted the other until he calmed. She was very tired. Indian women where expected to resume all activities and chores after childbirth, but the truth was that they helped each other unbeknownst to the husbands and captors. Childbirth was as painful and exhausting to them as it was to women around the world.

Even as she fed the babies, several warriors grumbled about her failure to start cooking. Little Crane stood from her father's lap and moved to build a fire. Tall Tree felt great pride in her and asked her if he could help.

She nodded and said, "Well, yes, you can. Mamma never let me cut meat because she said I was so clumsy I might cut my own hand off, so you can do that. Also, she would not let me cut the branches for the spit because of the knife. I can put the meat over the fire once the spit is in place. And I can turn it, too, so it does not burn."

Tall Tree watched his daughter and wished her mother could see her now. She looked so tiny as she dragged a water skin from the creek that the men smiled and offered to help her, too. She solemnly agreed, again making her father proud as well as her uncle Soaring Eagle. He let her select the branches for the spit, and then he cut them. She carefully assembled them, tying them with the sinew from the buffalo meat. When it was in place, old Man of Horses set the fire. Soon the camp smelled of roasting meat.

* * * *

Another time, Little Crane thought, maybe Summer Swan would show her how to find roots and berries for cooking as her mamma had done.

Thoughts of her mamma brought tears to her eyes, so she ran to where the Summer Swan dozed while feeding the babies. The woman opened her eyes and smiled at the child. "Would you like to hold one of them while I feed the other?" Little Crane smiled and held out her thin arms. "These two are quite a handful. Maybe your father will let you help me again sometimes."

"I am sure he will. I will drive him crazy until he says I can. It's taken my whole life to learn this, but it works every time."

Her whole life, all five years of it, thought Summer Swan, smiling. She was sure the child would win, as females of all ages learn to do. She dozed again and awakened when she heard footsteps. She turned to see Soaring Eagle carrying a chunk of meat on a stick. He handed it to her and left without saying a word. She realized she was ravenous and consumed it like a starving animal. She wrapped the babies tightly and lay beside them. She was asleep in minutes. She did not know when Little Crane joined them, snuggly close on the other side of the twins. Nor did she hear any of the discussion of her fate and that of the twins when the men gathered around the fire.

Chapter 7

Tall Tree spoke first. "Man of Horses, you are the eldest. We have no chief and need one. Please give us you thoughts."

Man of Horses squatted and puffed on his old pipe. "You are wrong, Tall Tree. We *do have* a chief. He is there," pointing with his pipe stem at Soaring Eagle. "My brother Cold Wind is gone, so his son is now our chief."

Immediately voices rose until they were shouting at each other. Man of Horses waited until they calmed down and continued. "That is the way of our people. I know many of you think it is because of him and his children that the gods have punished us. It was wrong for him to kill Hook Nose. I would have done the same thing if someone, even the Medicine Man, tried to slay my infants. In your heart of hearts, who can say honestly you would have done differently?'

Only Little Bear stood. Man of Horses stared at him for a long while until the young brave became nervous under the eyes of the elder. "How can you say what you would have done, Little Bear? You are married but have no children. The bond between a man and his wife is less than the bond between a man and his son. Is your wife important to you?"

Little Bear's voice was shrill and full of anger. "My wife is dead. He and his sons angered the gods and my beautiful wife paid for it. This will not end until Soaring Eagle and those devil children die, as did all of the others."

No one argued with him. Many felt the same way. "Do you think the death of Soaring Eagle and his sons will bring back those have perished? Will it stop the pain and suffering of those women over there? You want to take away his living children when he has already lost his wife and daughters, his mother, father and sisters? Who has lost more than he has?

"Our tribe has been decimated and we must keep those who are left. Without Soaring Eagle, who will bring down the most buffalo? Who can control our restless allies? Who has held off more of our enemies then all others? If you can answer those questions, then tell me. Otherwise, I proclaim the son of Cold Wind to take is place as our chief. Anyone object?"

There were some murmurs, but no outright comments. Soaring Eagle's eyes were on the fastened to the prone figures on the blanket where his sons, niece, and the wet woman slept. He had not lifted his eyes once during the discussion. Now he raised his eyes to those around him, slowing looking into each face. "Any who object, state so now. For after this campfire if I am your chief, I will be the Chief in all things, as my father Cold Wind was." No one spoke.

"So be it. Now, Man of Horses, I ask you as my revered uncle to name my sons."

"I will accept this honor and think on it tonight. I will tell you the names in the morning."

The men moved away from the fire to where their wounded lay. Tall Tree smiled at the place his daughter rested, then nodded at Soaring Eagle. Soon the camp was silent but for the crackling of the fire. Soaring Eagle walked to look down at his family on the buffalo blanket before beginning a watch over the camp. In a few hours, he would awaken another warrior to take his place, and then he could sleep.

Chapter 8

Morning began before dawn when two pair of robust little lungs announced hunger pangs. Little Crane was already in search of soft leaves to use for diapers that she tied around the kicking feet with sinew. Summer Swan lifted her shirt and put one hungry mouth to each tit. Watching her from the dark were several warriors. The younger, unmarried ones were enthralled with her huge, dark tipped breasts and long legs. Those whose wives were gone looked at her, wondering if she would eventually choose a mate from among them.

She approached Soaring Eagle and asked permission to go downstream to wash herself. He growled at her. "Do as you wish. You are a free woman, not my slave. All I want from you is your milk for my sons." With that, he turned away as if angry.

She shrugged off his abruptness, left the camp and walked until she found a sandy shore where she removed all her clothing. She moved into the water that was warmer than she had expected. It felt wonderful to wash. She used ashes from the fire pit to scrub her body and hair, and then rinsed it all away. Once clean, she lay on her back, letting the current move her into the middle of the creek before she rolled over and swam gracefully back to the beach.

Sitting in the water, she ran her fingers through her hair to remove the tangles. Some cattail plants grew near her, so she picked one and used it to brush her hair even smoother. She then braided it, adding a spray of flowers as she reached the ends.

A snap in the wooded area behind her caused her to freeze. She felt no sense of danger, so slowly arose, still naked, and turned to look in that direction. Two figures began to run away and she smiled. No normal man could pass up a chance to see a woman in her bath. No matter, she did not care who it was, but she did hope it might have been Soaring Eagle. No, she told herself, he would never spy and she was right.

She was beautiful by any standards, tall, slender, and graceful. She had been married and was no inexperienced girl. She knew those watching her would have erections. She hoped they were so hard they hurt, it might teach them a lesson.

Once back in camp, she knew within minutes who it had been, as neither of the younger warriors would even look in her direction. She made a point of walking near them and asking just loud enough for them to hear. "Did you enjoy my bath as much as I did?"

Chapter 9

At first light, Summer Swan awoke before the babies. She relieved herself behind a row of low bushes and gathered more leaves to catch the after-birth flow, which she noted was diminishing already. Probably due to the nursing of the boys, she decided. She moved toward the fire when she heard a voice behind her.

"You are here only to tend my children and Little Crane. You will stay with them and others will bring up water and do the cooking. If you want to watch over the other children while we hunt, you may do so. It is your choice. Perhaps the injured women can assist you, but other than that, your responsibility is my family. Is that understood?" Soaring Eagle's voice was cold and definitely an order.

"You yourself said I could do as I wish, that I am not your slave. And I wish now to help with the camp and cooking. When the little ones want me, I will return to them. Otherwise, I will do as I choose." She walked away, pulled a chunk of buffalo from its wrapping, and deftly slid in onto the spit before stoking the low fire. Within minutes, the meat began to sear and the aroma woke many of the others. A tiny cry called her back to the sleeping robes where she sat enjoying the tug and mouth on her breast.

Man of Horses approached her and sat on the sleeping robe looking at the children. A stern-faced Soaring Eagle joined them, taking care to look only at the boys, never at Summer Swan. "Last night in my dreams, the gods came to me with the names of your sons." The old man picked up one twin and held it high in both his hands as if showing it to the sky and gods. "This child will grow taller and slimmer than his brother. He will be strong, but mild in manner.

None will surpass his hunting skills or his speed in running. He will understand the animals and birds of the plains and kill only for food and cover, never for fun as some warriors do. I name him Land Hunter."

He looked at Soaring Eagle. "You gave me the privilege of naming your sons, but I want to know you accept these names. Both of you."

"What do you, both of us? The woman has nothing to do with it. She is only a source of food. Nothing more. And, in the past, the mother is never consulted where the name is concerned, nor the father either. It is the grandfather's choice only."

Man of Horses's face tightened. "Soaring Eagle, there is no grandfather, so I am consulting you for approval of my choices, the choices given to me by the gods. Without her, your children would have perished. It is her strength that feeds them. They are as much part of her as they are of you. It is time you understand that and accept that She Who Smiles is gone. You trust Summer Swan to feed and care for your sons. You must also trust her to be part of their lives for as long as she wants to remain with them. So, say no more about that.

"Now, is this child to be called Land Hunter?" Soaring Eagle said yes. Man of Horses looked at the woman who barely moved her head in a nod, eyes still on the child in her arms.

"So he shall be. The child," he picked up the other one, "will not be as tall as his brother, but he will be stronger. He will outwrestle every man who tries to best him. His skills in battle will become well known. His temper will be easily fired, but he will put it to rest as easily as it arises. He will be full of stealth and see things others do not. My name for him is Iron Eyes."

He looked from one adult to the other and both nodded. Soaring Eagle stalked away but Man of Horses remained, watching her as the children kicked at her side. "Summer Swan, he does not mean to cause you pain. His hurt is so deep he sees the entire world through it.

Slowly it will soften into wonderful memories and he will start living again. Be patient with him." She arose and moved away to help load the horses for the day's journey.

Summer Swan did not understand why she should be patient. Had not she also lost her husband and a child. He should be patient with her, not the other way around. Besides, she was feeding the babies out of her love of children and he had nothing to do with it at all. The next time he was rude to her, she would set him straight.

Her chance came sooner than expected, that very afternoon.

Chapter 10

She now carried the children on her back; together in a large pack that two of the recovering women helped her create. In it first went clean leaves and a layer of moss followed by more leaves and more moss and a layer of soft grasses. The children sat atop the packing below and freely passed their water and bowel movement. When the packing was soiled, it was easily replace by new at each stop.

The wounded women adored the boys and volunteered to take turns carrying them, but Summer Swan said no, but agreed that they could when they regained their strength. None of the injured was able to do more than stay on their horses, and one could not even manage that. She was Sweet Flower, who lay on a travois, unconscious and unaware that a horse pulled her to where ever they were going.

It was hot for Summer Swan and even hotter for the infants on her back. She stopped and dismounted her horse under a shaded tree. She slid the backpack off and laid it on the ground. She opened it to allow air to move over their sweating bodies. "Hey, little ones. I thought that Indian babies were a hardy bunch and did not cry at discomfort. So, why are you crying? I know you are not hungry and the only wetness I feel is your sweat." She smiled as she wiped their red bodies with water from her water bag, and then tickled their bare tummies, loving the tiny smiles she got.

She heard his horse coming at a full run, but she did not turn to greet him as he hit the ground before the horse even stopped completely. "What are you doing? Have you lost what little mind your have? Why are you stopping? There are enemies all around us, if you do not care about yourself, at least try to care for my babes. If that is too hard for you to handle, then I will do it myself."

Summer Swan stood, turned and walked as close to him as she could get without touching him. Then, touch him, she did. She began tapping his chest with her finger as hard as she could while she spoke, allowing her temper to build as she vented.

"It should be apparent to even an imbecile like you that I am stopping because the babies are so discomforted. It is too hot for them in the pack made of the wrong materials, but that is all we have. So, they need air and water to cool them. As for enemies, this is the first I have heard of it. If they are around, then why did you give no warning? Because you just made that up to frighten me. Well, it does not! The only thing around here that frightens me is you. You do not have a clue about babies. Even a male prairie dog knows more than you do. So you think you can do better than I do, then do it. If that is the way you want it, then fine with me."

She stepped back and swung up onto her horse. With heels in its sides, she raced away, in the opposite direction from the tribe as it moved closer to the buffalo herd, which scouts spotted that morning.

* * * *

Soaring Eagle stood like a rock statue. He could not believe she was leaving his sons to fend on their own. No, not leaving his sons, leaving him. He realized he had royally messed up, but pride stopped him from calling her back. He fastened the boys tightly into their pack, but laid it across his lap as he rode toward the tribe. The sun was directly overhead and its blinding light caused immediate tears from the little brown eyes. He tried to tip the pack out of the sun, but it did not help. Finally, he turned them upright, facing his chest. They continued to bawl even harder as his heat radiated to them.

His frustration level was at a boiling point when he reached the others. He called a halt as he stopped under a small tree for shade and uncovered them as *she* had. In his mind, *she* was a devil sent to plague him. Things worsened as Little Crane came running. "Where is Summer Swan? What have you done with her?" The injured women, barely able to walk, came toward him, shouting the same questions. Even the warriors wandered toward him, eyes wide and curious.

"I did nothing to her. She left on her own. She is a cruel woman who cares only about herself."

Little Crane was cried as she pounded his legs with her little fists. "She would never leave the babies. She loves them more than anyone does. Without her, they will die of hunger." She turned and ran to her father, who picked her up in his long arms. "Please, make him got find Summer Swan. Please, please?" She continued to cry until hiccups took over and her nose ran slime down her face.

Tall Tree looked at his brother-in-law. "Listen to the child. She is right. How are you going to feed them, or care for them? We need to hunt at dusk and we need you with us. The women are too hurt to care for the babies and Little Crane can do only so much. So, whatever you did to drive her away, you need to undo it. For your sons' sake."

"What is the matter with you all? A few days ago, you did not even want her with us. Now, somehow, she is some kind of human god. Well, let me tell you, she is not a god, she is not perfect, and she is mean and spiteful. No, I will not search for her."

Little Crane wiggled down from her fathers arms and ran to her horse which she led to a rock to make her high enough to mount. "Then, I will find her." She rode as fast as she could without bouncing off the horse.

"Damn it, I will go find her."

Tall Tree shouted after Soaring Eagle as he sped away. "Don't come back without Little Crane or you will answer to me."

Soaring Eagle caught up with Little Crane in less than a minute. He scooped her off her horse as he rode past. He knew her horse would return to the tribe. "Why are you so mean to Summer Swan?"

the child asked as she snuggled against his broad chest. "She is such a nice person and I love her. It is hard to love you, though, when you are mean to her. So why are you so mean?"

He looked down at her tear-stained face and felt a wave of guilt. Hell, he had hurt his sweet little niece for no reason other than his own inner anger. "You are right, my little kitten, I was wrong to yell at her. Let's go find her and bring her back "

"But what if she won't come back? If you yelled at me like that, I would never, never, never come back."

"Even if the babies needed you, you would not come back?"

"Well, for the babies I would come back, but not for you. You do not deserve it. Oh, look, there she is."

Indeed there she was, floating a small creek behind some bushes on the bank that did little to cover her. He could see her large breasts like balls on her chest and the dark Y where her legs joined. Against his iron will, he felt a stirring in his groin anyway.

"Oh, Summer Swan. There you are. We have come to take you home. But can I swim with you first? Can I, please, can I? Can I?"

"Yes, Little Crane, I would love to have you swim with me. But it is up to your uncle as he is the man in charge of everything. You will have to ask him."

"Not now, Little Crane. The babies need us. But I promise to bring you back later. Maybe your father would like to come, too."

"Only if Summer Swan can come back with us."

Summer Swan had waded out, not attempting to hide her nudity, and dropped her shirt over her head and stepped into her skirt. Her hair was still wet and her face and arms glistened with droplets in the sun. "We shall see, Little Crane, later. Anyway, come and you can ride back with me if your uncle apologizes otherwise you will have to go with him."

"Well, can I wade while he 'pologizes?"

"That is up to him, also."

Soaring Eagle nodded and waited until the youngster was in the water before he spoke softly. "I am sorry. I should not have shouted at you."

"I can't hear you, way up on that horse. I am down here."

He gritted his teeth up dismounted. "I am sorry," he said again.

"You are so far away; I cannot hear you very well."

Soaring Eagle took a deep breath and walked slowly to within a two feet of her. "Can you hear me now? I am sorry I yelled at you. The babies need you, so please come back."

"I accept that apology, such as it was. Be forewarned, though, that anything like this happens again, I will leave. As much as I love the children, I will not be treated like a slave ever again. Do you understand?"

He nodded. She turned to call the now soaking wet Little Crane. Summer Swan mounted her horse and Soaring Eagle settled his niece in front of her. The woman urged her horse into a run, calling out over her shoulder, "Last one back is a smelly skunk." He could hear the laughter ahead of him and smile as he urged his horse after them, making sure they arrived before he did.

Chapter 11

The entire tribe traveled with the warriors, the hunters. A normal situation would have the women, children, and old men staying in the village, but they had no village. Nor could they make one until they had buffalo skins for tepees, clothing, and shoes. The meat would need to be smoked and dried for later use. Their first order of business was finding the buffalo and hunting for meat to trade until they could smoke their own.

They searched for two days before a scout found a herd only a few hours ride away. During that time, they did find some deer, a few rabbits, and wild roots and plants to season their food. The deerskins would make soft dresses for the women and children and even a shirt or two for the men during the cold winters. However, more importantly, there would be shoes for all.

With the buffalo so close, the group urged their horses into faster gaits to arrive and establish camp before the hunt. The travois bounced with the pace of the horse pulling it, causing the rider, Sweet Flower to moan in pain. Summer Swan begged to ride slower for the woman's sake. Soaring Eagle merely shook his head no. He knew Summer Swan and his Little Crane would think him heartless, but the good of all was more important that the one injured woman, who he thought would die anyway.

When they came to a rise, the scout stopped them. "It is a small herd, restless, too. The sky looks like storm and they will stampede if it thunders. We have little time, I think."

There was no further discussion beyond Soaring Eagles command to those not hunting. "Here, you will build our camp. Have a smoking fire ready, too, as we have need meat and robes to trade and for our own use." He turned and silently the hunters rode over the rise and down toward the herd. The wind was in their favor, so the buffalo did not smell them. They readied their bows and arrows, taking their time approaching the massive animals.

Their luck held. Tall Tree's first arrow went true, reaching the bull's heart located behind the shoulders. The animal dropped like a huge brown rock that caused no concern among the others. Encouraged by Tall Tree's success, Little Bear shot and his aim was perfect, too. A second bull fell to the ground. The scout's arrow was off, hitting a buffalo in his stomach, causing a huge roar of pain. That sound and the smell of blood now alerted the others who began to run, in circles at first, giving the hunters more time for more arrows. Soaring Eagle downed two and Tall Tree a second one. Several more arrows hit others and the herd found a leader to follow, leaving the dead and wounded on the ground just as the first peal of thunder shook the plain.

They were pleased with their success. Six lay dead and five unable to rise. The hunters killed them quickly stop the animals' pain. It had all happened so quickly that Soaring Eagle sent one of the young men back to camp, instructing them to move the camp down to the killing field. Processing the dead creatures would be easier if they did not have to drag them or skin them another place.

* * * *

Summer Swan found herself in the strange position of directing up the camp. She, a former slave, was now in charge and the old men gave her advice, but not orders. No, never again would she bow to any captor. She would stay a free woman or die.

Only the fire circles were complete when the hunter arrived with news they were to move. Everyone mounted his horse and rode to where the men had started skinning the dead. Normally, the women did this work, but there were not enough women to do it all. Only Summer Swan and Little Crane were unhurt, but She Who Cries and Dark Woman (who was a slave) mended enough to gather rocks for the fire circles and wood for the fires. The smaller children picked up buffalo chips for warming fires. Sweet Flower on her travois asked to watch the twins as the other toiled. Summer Swan laid them beside her and bent to kiss her cheek and pat her head before returning to the tasks of setting up camp.

The river where she had bathed just days before was nearby so Little Crane led the horses to drink. It was not long before she ran back to where her father was cutting a buffalo into large chunks. "Father, Father. There are others away up the river. It is a large camp with hundreds of tepees. Where can we hide? I am so afraid." She had her arms wrapped around his legs and her face hidden against him. He lifted her and carried her to Summer Swan. "Keep her safe. She will tell you why. We will go to see what she found." Cold Wind, Tall Tree, and Soaring Eagle rode toward the river, then dismounted and walked. They disappeared into the trees while everyone watched.

Finally, Summer Swan regained her sense of necessity and quietly urged them to get back to the jobs of building a camp. By the time, the men returned the smoking fires blazed and over them hung large pieces of meat on tripods build over the fire. Once the fat and sinew of the animals was scraped from the inside of their pelts, the skins would be draped over the tripod, holding in the heat and smoke while the meat cured. The smoke tents were miniature tepees. Cooking fires were doing their jobs, too, and the aromas made stomachs growl with hunger.

This was the time when women got little rest. Their lot in life meant processing the bounty in many ways. They hung strips of meat on racks or tripods to dry in the hot sun or over a smoky fire to make jerky that would nourish them through the lean times and was perfect for hunters or scouts away for long periods. Sausages made from strips of meat and fat seasoned with wild onions and sage hung to dry.

Dried meat beaten with a rock until it turned to powder that when mixed with melted fat and berries became pemmican. In this form, it would last for months.

Berries, eaten fresh or dried and stored in birch bark containers also became dyes, jewelry, and medicines. Plants like wild rice, bitterroot, and prairie turnips became part of their stores. There were turnips eaten raw, boiled, or roasted. Dried turnips when pounded into flour and missed with grease collected from the bones of the animals became bannock, a type of bread cooked over a fire.

* * * *

Dusk had fallen when the three men came out of the trees and mounted their horses. They were smiling as they rode into camp. Tall Tree jumped from his horse and pickup up his little daughter. "You are the best scout in the camp, Little Crane. No one else so much as noticed the other camp. If they had been an unfriendly bunch, we might have had a repeat of the last attack.

"Instead, we have found a friendly tribe. They are willing to trade blankets and pelts for our fresh meat. And, if we can get them more, they might even be willing to part with a female slave or two. There are also several women in need of husbands, so you young bucks might give some thought to that."

Soaring Eagle sent out his scout again in search of buffalo. "Our new friends will be here tomorrow for meat. They invited us to move our camp near theirs and we think that is a good idea. It will be safer for our women and children while we chase the buffalo. But first we must complete this hunt."

Summer Swan had misgivings about such a move and spoke to the council of her hesitation even without tangible evidence that it was a wrong thing to do. "Can I speak?" she asked from her sitting position with the other females, a bit away from the inner circle of men.

Soaring Eagle looked at the male faces and saw no objections. "Summer Swan, you have permission to voice your opinion."

She stood and moved closer to the center of the tribe. "I cannot say why I think this is a mistake, but I do. Perhaps it is intuition, or a stray thought from the Gods or the spirits of our dead, but the idea of moving in with an unknown people causes my heart to beat faster and my head to fill with strange cries and visions of pain. It is usually for safety that people join together, but perhaps we would be unwise to do so without knowing more of the tribe before making such a change. Might we not be like the rabbit invited into the wolves den?

She nodded to each warrior as she looked around the circle, and they turned to return to the babes and her sleeping robes. The council decided to stay where they were, each man trusting the strange woman's insights.

Chapter 12

There was much excitement in camp that night. No one seemed to mind taking turns stoking the smoking fires. Little Crane had not forgotten the half-promise of a swim in the river, so began to beg Summer Swan, Soaring Eagle, and Tall Tree to take her. She finally convinced her father and the woman to accompany her, but Soaring Eagle declined. He claimed to have too much to do before the others arrived in the morning, but Summer Swan knew he declined because of her. But, she did not care. The cool water of the river would be wonderful after such a hot, sweaty day and she did not intend to miss a chance to be clean again. She nursed the babies and set out on her horse, riding with Tall Tree and Little Crane.

* * * *

Soaring Eagle felt a sense of anger, at what he was not sure. He did not like the idea of her naked body in the water with Tall Tree, but that was none of his business. If she wanted to flaunt her curves and temptations to Tall Tree, who was he to care?

But he did care. He knew he did. He remembered her floating in the water, hair spread around her, huge breasts, hard nipples, long legs, and curly black hair. He pictured himself between those legs, his cock buried in the black hair, and his mouth on hers. The picture in his mind caused him to harden until his penis hurt.

That night, she lay playing with the babies across the tent floor from him blowing on tiny tummies until little laughter erupted from deep within his sons. The sounds made both Summer Swan and

Soaring Eagle laugh. Her long hair fell to the sides of her face and the babes grabbed handfuls and tugged. She talked to them as only a woman can and he smiled. He watched the firelight flicker on her skin. Her nipples were still hard from the babies' mouths. He rolled over and feigned sleep, even emitting a soft snore, until she was sure he was asleep. She threw off her blanket and stepped outside to relieve herself.

When she returned, she lay uncovered. The moon rose and emitted lighted through the smoke hole in the top of the tepee. He could see her clearly though his slitted eyelids. By the Gods, she was beautiful. His stirring penis brought thoughts of She Who Smiles and with those thought, knowing that his wife would want him to love again, or at least find a relief for his needs. And such a relief was a scant few feet away.

When he was sure Summer Swan was asleep, he arose and walked to her. Standing over her lovely body, his penis grew rock hard and throbbed. He knelt beside her and bent to kiss her. Instead of compliant lips in return, he received a hard punch in his chest.

"What do you think you are doing? I am not yours. Get away from me. Or I swear I will leave this tent this minute and not return."

He dropped to his back, lying beside her. "You are so damn beautiful. How could any man ignore you? Do you not have needs, too? We can help each other and enjoy the pleasures the gods gave to us."

"You are the most arrogant, stupid, unthinking man I have ever met. Is this your way of approaching a woman, of inviting her to your bed? Well, you are sorely mistaken if you think I am interested at all in pleasures with you. Now, get away. I mean it."

Soaring Eagle did not move. "I will move away if you give me a chance to please you. I promise. If you do not like my touches and caresses within time it takes the moon to move away from the smoke hole, I go back to my sleeping robes. But if you do, will you be honest enough to admit it to me and to yourself?"

When she did not answer, he raised himself up on one elbow and let his head bent over her body. His tongue touched the end of her nipple as his free hand moved to envelope her other breast. He tasted the milk that she provided for his sons and that excited him even more. His lips encircled her nipple and he gently suckled it, feeling it harden in his mouth.

His free hand moved down to rub her stomach, then her hips. The woman smell of her excited all his senses. His tongue followed until she pulled his head up and met his lips with her own. There was no doubt that they would couple and it would be good.

His fingers moved between her legs, sliding into the wetness there. She moaned in her throat as he touched her clit. He began to rub it and felt it growing. She opened her legs wide and pushed her hips up to meet his hand. She held his head to her breasts as she began jerking side-to-side, up and down, whispering 'more, more, more' until she dropped back on the sleeping robe.

He knelt between her knees, lifting her buttocks up as he slowly pushed inside her. His excitement built too fast for him to control and his semen spurt into her like a flood. She held him to her, inside her, and raised her lips to his again as he dropped down atop her sweating body.

They rested, saying not a word nor moving, until they both felt his cock wiggling again. This time, he moved at a slower pace. She wrapped her long legs around his hips and met his every thrust. They shared endless kisses and touches as their fever mounted. She felt his long cock deep within her and let her body go with the feelings it aroused. His mind now knew nothing but her pussy and his penis; his body took over. They rode together to a sensual crest, each murmuring words, but not words of love. Words of lust. Demands for pleasure. He whispered that he could not hold off any more. She lifted her hips high and moaned her climax as he met his.

Again they rested without speaking, listening to their breathing slow back to normal. Then, she pushed him off her and moved her head to his hips. She took penis into her mouth until it began to grow again. He moaned and begged her to stop, which she did not do. His hands held her head, his hips jerked, and he released as much cum as he had the first two times, amazing them both.

She tried to push him away, but he reached once again between her legs. The wetness from her excitement and his cum ran down into her butt crack. He rubbed there first, then up into her vagina, using three fingers to rub the top of her canal. Suddenly she cried out and he knew he had found the spot, the spot She Who Smiles enjoyed above all else.

Soaring Eagle arose and left the tent. By the time he returned from relieving himself, she was asleep. He wanted to return to her for what he and She Who Smiles had called his dessert, but that would have to wait until another time. He dropped to his bed and slept.

Chapter 13

Summer Swan had never experienced anything that felt like that did. It was as if a hundred clits were exploding at the same time, over and again, while she cried out her ecstasy. She fell exhausted on her sleep robe. In what seemed like a few minutes, rather than hours, she awoke to two pair of kicking feet prodding her hips. She fed the boys and smiled as she recalled the night of pleasure they had enjoyed. She washed herself and the twins as best she could, dressed, and carried Land Hunter and Iron Eyes outside to meet the world.

She could not see Soaring Eagle anywhere, but the camp was full of men and a few women who she knew were from the other tribe. She moved forward, introduced herself to them, and soon was deep in discussion with the women regarding the twins, tanning hides, and what was considered women's work.

The day was wondrous with so many new folks to meet and enjoy food. The new friends brought much to share including currant berries and wild onion stew. The men laughed, talked, and bartered into the night. There was much discussion in whispers about the twin sons of the chief, but no one dared question their being alive and not killed at birth. Women, as all women will do, took turns holding the babies.

Much trading occurred with pleasing results on both sides. Their abundance of meat gave them robes and skins. Summer Swan traded some of her herbs and roots for theirs, along with instructions on their uses. Each tribe was pleased with the results

There were also several young women and naturally, the young men were especially glad of that. It was unlikely any real attachments would develop so soon, but it gave all the warriors hope for wives since their own village now had so few women. Even the older warriors seemed more attentive this day. Perhaps romance was in the air. Summer Swan smiled to herself, remembering the night she and Soaring Eagle shared.

That smile diminished after she changed the boys and fed them hopefully for the last time until morning. Soaring Eagle did not return until very late and fell to sleep immediately on his own sleeping robes. The next night was the same. And the third. Summer Swan finally had to accept that she was just a convenience for him to get relieve from over full balls and a stiff penis. Well, next time there would be no next time.

The warm days on the plains began to turn colder. By now, there were back at the original camp, beside the river, below the Witness Tree. Life was good. Dark Woman and She Who Cries both had new husbands, and even Sweet Flower had a suitor. Sweet Flower spent most of her time, sitting while her tortured legs grew stronger, but she was never bored because all the children gravitated to her. They sensed her goodness and her love and adored her in return.

The twins were trying to walk to the enjoyment of everyone. Little Crane took each by one hand and the trio walked slowly around the camp, until something or someone caught the attention of the little eyes. They would drop her hands and scurry away on hands and knees until their reached their goal or something else caught their fancy.

Summer Swan knew it was time to wean them from her breasts, but she enjoyed their nursing. She promised herself it would stop when they walked, which she knew would be soon. She vowed to withhold her breasts, allowing her milk to diminish, and to teach the boys to drink from the cups she and Little Crane made for them out of hollowed limbs. They liked their cups, but at bedtime, they wanted her tits. She sighed deeply, starting tonight, she told herself.

That evening things worsened. First, the charming twins were overly tired from hard play with Little Crane. Second, they did not want their cups. Third, they cried and crawled all over her, trying to get to her breast. Fourth, Soaring Eagle came in and began laughing as his sons bombarded her from every direction.

"Stop laughing and help me," Summer Swan yelled at him.

"What do you want me to do? I do not have tits for them to suckle, so what can I possibly do to help?"

"You can grab one of them and hold him down while I try to feed the other one from his cup. Or better yet, I will hold one and you feed the other."

He grinned. "That does not seem like much of a problem." He picked up one of the milk-filled cups and pressed it to the lips of the child on his lap. Land Hunter grinned up at his father and drank several swallows. Iron Eye watched his brother and began to cry, struggling to get away from Summer Swan. She let him go and watched as he crawled on fleet hands and knees until he also sat on his father. Soaring Eagle gave him a couple swallows before returning it to his brother. They took turns and when the cup was empty, fussed until he started with the second one. They slowed in their drinking and began rubbing their eyes, a sure sign they were sleepy.

Summer Swan picked up Land Hunter and carried him to a spot she had prepared for them to sleep, away from her breasts. Soaring Eagle carried Iron Eyes and placed him beside his brother. Neither child was happy about the arrangement and whimpered his displeasure. Summer Swan patted each on his back until they settled into sleep.

When she tried to rise, she found herself locked in the arms of a determined man. She could feel his penis pressed against her as he pushed her down and lay atop her, trying to kiss her as he squeezed her breast.

* * * *

At that very moment, Little Crane ran into the tepee without warning, a cardinal sin in their tribe, carrying two pair of small shoes.

"I got these done just in time. It is starting to snow and..." she stopped and her eyes grew large. Her uncle was on top of Summer Swan. She knew that is what men and women did, she had seen her mother raped and all her life watched animals mate. She turned and ran back outside. Within seconds, she was back. "I understand. You are going to get married. Right? Oh, that is wonderful." She jumped up and down in her excitement.

"No, Little Crane, we are not getting married," her uncle said. He arose and moved to sit on his buffalo skin. He picked up the child and sat her in his lap. "I like Summer Swan a great deal, but not to marry. I will not marry again. She Who Smiles will always be my wife."

"But you laid on her, like married people do. It is not right for you to lie on her any other way. My mother told me that and my father agrees. If you are not going to marry her, then you should not have laid on her like that. You are bad, Uncle." She wiggled out of his grasp and ran outside, throwing the tiny shoes at him as she left.

Summer Swan did not move. His words were like a river of ice washing over her. In her heart of hearts, she was sure that one day he would take her as his wife. No, all he took from her was what his body needed, not his mind. She wanted to cry and scream but refused to let him see her hurt. She arose and began to gather her few personal belongings, which she dropped onto her sleeping robe. She rolled it up and walked to the door without a word.

In one step, he was beside her, holding her arm tightly in his hand. "Wait, let me explain."

She looked into his eyes without moving. He slowly released her arm and let his hand drop to his side. Without a word, she left the tepee.

Chapter 14

Summer Swan had no idea where she would go, but she was determined not to return to the tepee of Soaring Eagle. In her heart, she knew she loved him, now she admitted it to herself. She wanted to be his wife and raise his sons. They were as much a part of her now as they were of him. However, it was not to be.

She moved quietly as the first flakes of the season floated down around her. They melted immediately but were portends of the cold time ahead. She remembered a copse of small trees under the large mother tree on the hill and headed in that direction. She moved passed Tall Tree's home and heard soft crying inside. She tapped on the door and waited until he called "Enter."

She stepping inside Little Crane sat crying in her father's lap as he snuggled her close.

"Tall Tree, please. Can I talk to Little Crane? She is upset and I understand why?"

"I would like to understand why, as well," he said. "Please explain because in her tears and sobs, she is hard to understand." He moved his had to indicate she should sit.

Summer Swan took a deep breath. "It is hard to speak. We had been playing on my sleeping robe with the babies. When they finally fell asleep, Soaring Eagle turned to me and held me down with his body. He was…" Tall Tree nodded his understanding. "Little Crane mistook our play for something far different. She asked is we were getting married. Soaring Eagle explained that we were not and that he would never marry again.

"Little Crane," she said. "Will you come to me and let me explain." The child arose and sat on her lap. "It was a game we sometimes play, usually with the twins. It means nothing. Can I tell you a secret?" Little Crane nodded. "I have to wean the boys and the best way for me to do it is for me to give them no chance to suckle. So, I am going to move tonight and tomorrow I will build my own home. Would you like to help me?"

"Oh yes, Summer Swan. I would love to help you. Please, father, can I help?" He nodded. "And because she has no place to sleep tonight, can she share my sleeping robe?"

Again, he nodded. "Oh, that will be so much fun. Come on. Let us go to bed now. I am tired."

"You will have to work hard tomorrow to help Summer Swan, so close your little eyes and tell the gods what is in your heart. We will sit here by the fire and talk for a few minutes."

"I will, but hurry, Summer Swan. I love you so much. And you too, Father."

* * * *

The adults sat quietly, discussing the snow and the coming of winter. Soft snores came from the child. Tall Tree stood and offered her his hand to rise from the dirt floor. They stepped outside and walked to the edge of the camp where no one would hear them. They stood in the lightly falling snow. Summer Swan caught flakes with her tongue and hands like a child. Tall Tree smiled and watched her animated face. She was so beautiful, he thought for the millionth time. Soaring Eagle was dumber than a stump to let her slip out of his fingers. A dead wife would keep no one warm at night nor produce strong sons.

"Summer Swan, I have thought of you more times than you can imagine. I want a wife like you, but I felt you belonged to Soaring

Eagle. I can see now that it is not the case. Can we get to know one another better? Can I pursue you to that end? Will you consider me?"

She stopped chasing snowflakes and looked at him as if it was the first time she had ever seen him. "I cannot answer that question right now, but we can get to know each other better. I would like that, but we must not give Little Crane any ideas. She has enough of her own." They both laughed.

* * * *

Soaring Eagle stood outside his abode, in the shadows. He could not hear what they said, but he did hear the laughter. He felt as if someone had hit him in the stomach. His head swam with jealousy that he knew he had no to right to feel. He had rejected her and hurt her. He never thought she wanted to be more than a wet woman for his sons. Now she was gone and had already found another man. His anger at her and his brother-in-law built until he realized he had clenched his fists so hard they hurt. Who could blame Tall Tree? He was a virile man in need of a woman, just as he himself had needed a woman. What of Summer Swan? Did she hunger for a husband so badly that she would take the first to ask? He turned back into his tepee and lay unsleeping for hours, listening to the soft snores of his sons.

Chapter 15

The following morning was warm and all signs of the cold season had disappeared. Little Crane was awake before daylight. She whispered in a voice so loud she knew it would wake her father and Summer Swan. "Can we start right away? I know where the buffalo skins for tepees are stacked. Or should we cut branches for the frame first?"

"The first thing we should do is eat," chided her father. "That means starting a fire and setting up your little spit for meat. And then, if she wants your help, you can ask Summer Swan what she has planned. I will go cut the trees for the frames and bring the buffalo skins back myself. One thing that does need your young hands, my daughter, is for you to gather some boughs to sweep the area where Summer Swan wants her tepee."

Even the idea of sweeping did not lower the child's high spirit. "Oh, daughter, there is no need for you to tell anyone what is going on. That is for Summer Swan to do. Understood?"

She nodded and raced outside to start to assemble her little spit and gather buffalo chips to start the fire, then wood to roast the meat.

The two adults smiled shyly at one another and left the tepee one, then another, hoping she did not notice. Of course, they were not that lucky, as several children saw her and ran back to their parents to report.

Summer Swan helped Little Crane with the spit and wood. The child ran to her, taking her hand. "Where will we build your tepee? How about right here, next to ours? Why, we could even hook the two together, like some large families do."

"Hold up a bit, sweet child. I do not think that is a good idea. Actually, it would be better if my home were far away from the tepees of all the unmarried men, so people would not talk. I like the spot over by Man of Horse."

"But, Summer Swan, that is so far from ours. And whom will you talk to way over there? And you know, Father will not let me go that far at night. Please, please, be closer."

This time Summer Swan was firm. "I will talk to Man of Horses. He is so nice and so full of wonderful stories. I am sure I will never get tired of listening to him. And since he is alone, I wager that he would like to join me for some meals.

"And you are right; you should not be running around camp after dark, so you will come only during the day unless invited for the night. That will happen only once in a while. You need to be with young people."

Her face clouded. "The only young people are those babies. Not the twins, but the other ones who lived. And they are all boys. I don't like boys expect Iron Eyes and Land Hunter."

Summer Swan smiled at her. 'I have an idea. Look, there is She Who Cries and Dark Woman. They are not many years older than you are. Let us go speak to them." Little Crane hung back, but the woman would not release her hand.

The two young women smiled as they approached. She Who Cries started giggling, something they had never seen before. "I have great news, but do no tell anyone yet. I want to tell my husband first. Promise?" All three nodded. "I am going to have a baby. About the time of the first hot days next year, I think. When Curved Bear Claws comes home tomorrow, then I will tell him. He and some of the others are scouting for close herds of deer or buffalo."

Summer Swan hugged the girl. It was hard to think of her as a full-grown woman because her years numbered only fifteen, one less than Dark Woman. Little Crane could not take her eyes off their stomachs. "Dark Woman, do you have a baby inside you, too?"

"No, I don't think so. I am just a bit rounder all over than She Who Cries. I wish I did though. Then you could help me with it like you helped Summer Swan."

"I would like that. Can I help you, She Who Cries? I know all about babies. I almost saw one born one time, before my mother shooed me off."

The women smiled. "Little Crane, there is a lot to do when a woman has a baby in her stomach. She needs her back rubbed and sometimes her feet, too. She cannot lift things that are heavy when her stomach gets big and might need some help."

"How do you know so much, Summer Swan? You do not have children."

Pain at the loss of her child swelled up in her heart and soul. She answered slowly with tears forming in her eyes. "I did have a daughter. She was beautiful, just like you. But she died. That is when your uncle found me and brought me back to feed the hungry babies. Do you remember? Now we have jobs to do. You can come back and visit with Dark Woman and She Who Cries whenever they want you to."

"Oh, can I?" She looked at them and grinned when they nodded.

"Now, go, find those branches to sweep." She turned and smiled at the young women. "You may be sorry you agreed so readily. She can become a bit of a pest if you let her."

Dark Woman answered. "That is no problem. She reminds me of my little sister who died. I will enjoy her and it will be nice to have a sister again. If she wants to be."

Little Crane swept the ground clean, with the approval of old Man of Horses who was delighted to have company near him. When Tall Tree arrived with the small trees, buffalo sinew to tie the uprights together, and the tanned hides it took little time to erect her new home. The young women came to help and brought a couple of small cups and a pot for her to use.

Man of Horses supervised, making sure that the opening faced east, as all their homes did. He sent the small boys who were under foot out onto the prairie in search of rocks as big as they could carry, buffalo chips, and small wood pieces for her fire circle. By the time the sun was high, her home was complete. Soaring Eagle, with a son in each arm, nodded as he passed by to visit the old man next door. The twins wiggled to get at Summer Swan, so she went inside and fastened the door to keep them away from her. They whined and whimpered but finally gave up in search of something to put in their mouths. She did not worry because she heard Little Crane scolding them.

Now she was free of her responsibilities to Soaring Eagle and his sons, she would start doing her share of women's work. They had no skins to tan then, so she moved onto the plain in search of more herbs, roots, and shrubs to help heal. Some in the tribe already referred to her as the Shaman, the medicine man.

When she returned to her home at dusk, Man with Horses sat outside his tepee and motioned her to join him. He was blunt in his questions, but that is the way of the old, she thought.

"Why did you leave the tepee of Soaring Eagle?" he asked.

"Because my job there was finished. The boys are no longer in need of my milk."

"Did Soaring Eagle hurt you some way?"

"Not really. He has no need for a wife and I will never again be a slave to any man."

"Ah, you were once a slave?"

"Yes. My master was kind and married me, but his first wives hated me. He died in a buffalo hunt. When my child died at birth, I could not return to the tribe for fear of my life. Soaring Eagle found me and brought me with him. He told me I was free to leave if I wanted, but his sons needed me."

"Ah," said the old man, puffing on his pipe. "What will you do now? Do you wish to be a wife again?"

Summer Swan smiled at him. "Yes, if I find a man who pleases me. I will not marry just to have a husband. But, you need not worry; I will do my share of work for the tribe. Like today, I gathered medicines. Tomorrow, I will help sew deerskin garments as the weather is cooling and we will all need warmer things."

"Yes, that is true. But will you not be lonely?"

"No, Man of Horses. I have friends among the women, few that we are. I have the children to care for and love. Little Crane has no mother now, so she needs someone to teach her how to tan hides, sew, and what the prairie offers."

"That is all good, but you are a woman and women have other needs. You must be careful that you are not the cause for men to argue and fight. Horny men and a beautiful woman have caused many deaths. Sometimes a woman who does not wish to marry any of her suitors but who likes them, well, she can enjoy them on her robes at night. She can enjoy them together, to show no favoritism, which causes jealousy. Sometimes together is best. When I was young, I enjoyed those times. Later I married and shared my wife occasionally, if she agreed, and when she was willing. She liked it and it excited me to watch. You might want to think about this."

Summer Swan nodded to him. He continued his reminiscing. "She took her task of teaching the young warriors very seriously, but that was different than simply sharing with a friend or guest. Sometimes we would demonstrate to the young bucks to make sure they understood."

Summer Swan looked puzzled and asked, "What do you mean, teaching the young warriors? What did you teach them? What did you demonstrate? I have never heard of this before."

"This has been a tradition in our village for generations. The gods watched our early people from the sky and took pity on the women who dreaded and disliked the act of reproduction. The gods decided that women would be more productive and willing if the men were better at their part of the mating. So, they send a godly woman down to teach the men the things that women like and dislike. When the men learned to please their mates, they wanted all couples to be as happy with one another as the first lovers were.

"It was decreed that in each tribe a young, beautiful married woman should teach those who had passed their manhood trials how to please a female. That woman was usually the wife of a chief or another the chief picks if he is without a wife. It is common for his choice to be a slave that shares his life with him. When she catches a child from him, he usually marries her, but not always. If the woman chooses not to marry, she nourishes the child until it no longer needs her. She then leaves the child with its father and is free to move from man to man. If no other weds her, she dies a lonely old woman pitied by all. This is often the fate of women who like the cocks of too many men.

"Some of the young warriors were better at fighting and hunting than at loving, so the woman and her man might decide to demonstrate to them how it was done. No young man was allowed to join the warriors and hunters until he had learned all aspects of manhood."

Summer Swan smiled, and then laughed. "How many of those young men pretended ignorance to continue their lessons?"

Man of Horses was serious when he answered. "The woman would know and refuse him any more lessons. Her husband might also be aware of the ruse and kick out the young man. And kick, I mean. He would push him to the door, naked, and boot him out into the view of all people present. The young man would grin sheepishly and beg for his clothes, but he could not have them until the following morning. He was forced to run to where ever he had other attire, much to the pleasure of the giggling young women."

"How did the woman keep from catching a child from the young men?"

"Ah, simply. She taught them only when she was already with child from her husband or she taught them everything but the actual joining, which she and her man would show them. Besides, pregnant women get horny once their fear of getting that way is no longer a problem."

Summer Swan spent a great deal of time that night and in nights to follow, thinking of the pleasures a woman could receive while teaching young warriors how to make other women want to fuck. She smiled to herself and closed her eyes each night when she was alone, letting her mind set the scene and her hands bring her climaxes.

Chapter 16

Summer Swan did think about what he said to her, about laying with more than one man in the night. Or, maybe, she thought, even in the day. Maybe on the soft grass by the river. In the bright sun, warming their bodies. She felt her body stirring at the images her mind created. She forced the men to be faceless, but she could see their bodies, glistening with sweat in the sun. One kissed her breasts as the other knelt between her legs, lifting her hips, and burying his face in her curls. She lifted the head of the man at her breasts and kissed him deeply as her vagina moistened and her clit exploded. She took his penis in her hand and guided it to her mouth. Yes, she thought, this would be exciting. She let her mind return to her fantasy. The man between her legs slid his cock into her wet canal and watched as her lips and mouth moved on the other penis. Her insides began to quiver to the movements of both men. All three of them exploded at the same time.

Summer Swan opened her eyes, letting the visions fade away. She felt her womanhood tingling with want, which she tried to ignore. She could not and her hand moved down to touch her throbbing clit, moving it, rolling it, pressing it until her hips lifted from the robe as if to meet deep, hard strokes of her lover. Her climax left her breathing hard and wishing it had been a man instead of her hand. What man, she would have to decide, because she knew what she needed.

* * * *

A scout rode into the village shortly after dawn with the word that a large herd of buffalo was near. The village left its quiet day-to-day living and shifted into a flurry of activity. The hunters left, accompanied by the two old men who led the packhorses that would return with meat and skins.

The women carried buckets of water to the huge hollow tree trunk they used to soak the pelts where they would remain in the water for three to six days. Then they removed the fur and cut off the hair as close to the skin as possible. They were made of ashes that broke down the remaining hair, which they scraped away before starting the tanning process. If the fur was to remain on the pelt, they skipped the lye step. These pelts make sleeping robes and winter over-clothing. The same method is used for pelts of other game.

The entire process seemed endless to the few women who had so little time, that their other jobs suffered. Finally, Summer Swan suggested one evening that the men must help. Her idea met with grumbling and hoots until she said quietly, "In that case, not all the pelts will be completed before they rot. We women can do only so much and we have reached that point now."

In the morning, still grumbling and voicing their unhappiness, most of the warriors pitched in and soon found themselves actually enjoying the camaraderie with each other and the much-happier females.

Little Crane got her first real lesson in cutting meat and smoking it as well as the art of tanning hides. At first, she flitted between one task and the other, until the women tired of her annoying antics and asked Summer Swan to put her to doing something useful. The child did not like any part of it when told she had to actually work instead of play at working. As Summer Swan reminded her, in Little Crane's own words, "I am not a baby anymore. I am six summer's old and nearly a woman."

* * * *

The hunt was a success with eight more buffalo, which the hunters decided was as many as they could handle at a time. Everyone worked at every task, even the men who still thought only women did some of the tasks.

Soaring Eagle announced as they ate the first night after the hunt, "We have too few women to handle all the buffalo. If we are going to have enough to eat and keep us warm during the snow and cold, we must all help. If you do not help, you do not eat or share the blankets and clothes we make. The choice is yours." There were some mutters, particularly from the young, unmarried men, but that soon subsided when they realized he meant what he had said.

Every evening the people dropped exhausted on their sleeping robes. Only Soaring Eagle could not. In his tepee were two ever hungry, busy, crawling boys wanted only to play, not sleep. He would not ask for help, even if he could think of someone to ask. After an hour or two of playing, they would fall asleep, only to awaken in a couple hours for a drink that led to more play. How had She Who Smiles lived with the children at night and worked all day? He had no idea.

* * * *

The day the last of the meat and pelts were complete, the sun rose and heated the prairie, as it had not in nearly a moon. It lifted the spirits of all, especially Little Crane, who had already forgotten her anger with Summer Swan. "Can we go swimming today? I promise to be good."

"Well, if your father agrees. Perhaps others would like to join us, too. Remember, though, that the water will be a lot colder than it was last time, so bring something warm to wrap in for the ride back."

"Oh, I was hoping it would just be you and me and father. Like a little family."

"Sweet child, we are not a family, just three friends. So ask others if they want to come, also." A pout appeared on her face, but she nodded and ran back to the middle of the village, calling out an invitation for a swim.

Ten people including the three of them, Soaring Eagle and the twins, Dark Woman, She Who Cries and their husbands rode together to the river. She Who Cries spoke as she waded into the water up to her knees, "By the gods, I did not think it would be so cold. I think this is deep enough. I don't want my child born with icicles hanging from his nose." Her husband Curved Bear Claw laughed and picked her up in his arms. He waded out to his stomach, holding her up, threatening to drop her.

Little Crane was already naked and in the icy water. She ran to him, splashing water on everyone. "You stop that. You will hurt her and the baby. Take her to shore immediately, do you hear?"

He laughed and asked, "If I do not, what will you do?"

Little Crane thought a moment before answering, "There is nothing I can do right now, but you better watch out later. I may be little but I have a big memory and I will get you later."

Again, he laughed, but replied, "I believe you will. So, I will do as you ask. Please remember that I did what you wanted, so you don't have to revenge me later."

She nodded serious and watched as he walked ashore and set his wife on her feet.

She Who Cries buried her face against his chest to hide her laughter. "You better pray for a son, because imagine having a daughter like that. You will learn in short order who the boss will be."

He whispered, "I love it. I hope we have a daughter, after our sons, who is just like that." To the others he said, "My wife is cold, so I think I will take her home and warm her." She Who Cries was embarrassed as the others laughed and Tall Tree said he was sure she would be warm when her husband was done with the task.

The reference to warming was not lost on any of the others but the children. By now, Dark Woman was floating naked by her husband around the bend from the others and they decided 'warming' was needed too and rode quickly back to the village.

* * * *

The twins began fussing, as their little feet grew cold. At the same time, they saw Summer Swan's large tits on the surface of the water and wanted to get at them. Soaring Eagle understood their desire, because his desire was the same but for a different reason. He, too, wanted to feel the nipples in his mouth as he lay on her body, moving in and out, as they had before. Even in the cold water, his penis grew unbearably hard so he forced himself to look away. Little Crane cried she was cold, so Soaring Eagle told her to get on her horse and follow him and the boys back to camp. He wanted her with her father and Summer Swan, but her chattering teeth made him urge her to come with him.

Had there been any others swimming, he would have asked them if Little Crane could go back with them, but he was the one with the babies and had no choice but to go. Besides, what would he do with only Tall Tree and Summer Swan still here? He knew they would not welcome his presence.

* * * *

When the four rode away, Tall Tree swam to where floated. She looked up and him and smiled, breaking his reserve to stay away from her until she invited him. Amazingly, even in the icy water, his penis hardened as he looked at her. By the gods, she was beautiful. He stood in the shallow water and lifted her behind her back until she stood in front of him. Very slowly, never taking his eyes from hers, he lowered his head until their lips touched. It was like a bolt of lightning to him. She closed her eyes, ran her tongue around the inside of his mouth, and then began to suck his tongue. He moaned deep in his throat, a loud almost animal moan. He felt like an animal, in pain with the need to mate.

He picked her up in his arms, waded to the shore, and laid her down gently, dropping beside her. He kissed her again and felt her response when she pressed herself against him. Her tits pressed his chest and their nipples hardened from the cold or was it desire? He tried not to rush, but his need turned his control into nothing as he slid his cock into her and exploded almost immediately.

"I am sorry, Summer Swan. That is not what I wanted to do. I have not been with a woman since, please forgive me and let me really love you." She simply smiled at his and put her arms around his neck. He saw her hard nipples with drops of water, or maybe still milk, on them and lowered his mouth first to one, then the other. Nothing he had ever tasted was so sweet. He suckled them, which brought a deep sigh from her. He took that as a sign she granted him permission to begin caressing her entire body. His tongue moved down, down across her tummy, down even lower. His fingers opened her wetness, still dripping with his semen. Feeling himself in her was stimulus enough for him to harden again. Her hand found him and she slowly skimmed his penis up and down until he moved it away from her, afraid he would climax too soon again.

"Do you like this, beautiful woman?" He moved his fingers inside her, into her canal, drawing out the moisture. His fingers found her clit and pulled it gently. He rubbed it, watching her face as she began to breathe quickly. He kissed her lips and breasts as she moved. He knew she was close, but wanted to prolong it if he could. He slowed his movements inside her wetness and she slowed her. She opened her eyes and looked at him, her eyes questioning why he stopped.

"I am not stopping, sweet one. I am letting it rest for a moment, and it will be better now." He moved his fingers again slowly, but with much more pressure. She drew a deep breath and moaned. The more pressure he applied with the now quickly moving fingers, the more she responded. Her tits bounced and her hips rose to meet his hand. She cried out as the wave of pleasure took over her existence. She begged for more, more, more until she knew the crescendo was winding down.

"Now, Tall Tree! Please. Please. Put your cock in me again. I want to feel you." He did as she asked, moving slowly at first. He savored every stroke, even more so when she wrapped her arms and legs around him and met his every move. Together they increased their mating speed until their whole world was where they became one. Together they climbed the mountain and flew into heaven where only a joined couple can go.

* * * *

They lay in the sun, letting its warmth dry their sweaty bodies. Tall Tree rolled over to look into her face. "What do you see," she asked.

"What I see is a beautiful, wonderful, loving woman. If I could, I would mount you again until we climaxed forever, but I think my shriveled penis is not up to a forever climax. But, I want to make you reach the sky again." He moved his hand down into her curls, but she stopped him.

"I think it best if you let me recover, too. Now, for a quick bath and back to the village. People will wonder why we are so long."

Tall Tree sprang to his feet and pulled up her up against him. He laughed as he kissed her. "They already know why we are taking so long. What man in his right mind could resist when he watched your body in the water? And they are jealous, as I was when I was sure you were sharing your robes with Soaring Eagle."

"Whether or not I shared my robes with Soaring Eagle or anyone else is not your concern." He felt her pulling away from him, both physically and in her mind.

"I am sorry, Summer Swan. I meant no harm. Actually, I meant it as a compliment to let you know how I have desired you from afar since, well, for a long time. I am a man who needs a woman, a wife, if you will have me."

Summer Swan avoided his eyes. "I am not sure I am ready to marry, now or ever. Marriage is a kind of slavery and I will never be a slave again, as I have told you. That is why I have my own home, so that I am obligated to no man. What we shared was wonderful and we might do it again sometime, but not every night or every few nights, like married people do. I will mate only when I want to with who I want to. Do you understand?"

He nodded. This was not turning out the way he had dreamed. He kissed her head and released her. They washed and dressed in silence. It was nearly dark when they reached the village a short ride away. They tied up their horses with the others and walked to her tepee where she said a quiet 'goodnight' and closed the flap behind her.

She did not even light a heating fire nor ate anything. She wrapped up in her sleeping robes and fell to sleep immediately, never knowing that several pairs of eyes watched them as they parted for the night.

Chapter 17

"You were late last night, father. I waited for you to eat, but gave up. I was so hungry. What did you and Summer Swan do last night that took you so long?"

Tall Tree thought he should be getting use to her questions, but still had trouble accepting that she was not a baby any more. "We sat by the water and talked at first. Then listened to the creatures, and talked some more."

Little Crane jumped up and down, clapping her hands. "I know! You asked her to marry you. She will be my mother." She giggled and headed for the tepee exit.

"Hold it right there, daughter. Get back here and sit down." From his tone, she knew better than disobey him. "Now, listen, because this is all I am going to say about it. And you will say nothing beyond what I just told you, should anyone ask, which they will not, as it is not anyone's business but Summer Swan and mine.

"No, I did not ask her to marry me, so she could not say yes or no. I do not think now is the time for her to marry, nor for me either. When it happens, if it happens, you will be the first to know. Do you understand? There will be no talk about any of this. If there is, I will know where it came from and you know what will happen then, do you not?"

She nodded and dropped back into her sleeping robe and turned her back on him. He knew she was disappointed and that she wanted to cry. He suspected she would decide she was too big for that. He knew his daughter well and was sure she could and would do her best to see that the two of them got together.

Tall Tree slipped on his moccasins and left the tepee, calling to her as he did so. "Now, get your skinny little butt out here and help. There are chores to be done and your robes are not the place to do them." In his heart, he wished that what she guessed had been the truth and felt only a bit badly for lying to her. He wanted Summer Swan to be his wife, but if he had her at all, it would be on her terms only. Remembering their sex the night before caused his cock to stir. He wanted her again, right this minute, but would have to wait until she approached him. That was something he had never experienced before and it was not a pleasant feeling.

He knew, as did Summer Swan, all ignored what people did in their tepees. Sounds of lovemaking, arguments, and even physical abuse were private matters, never discussed, or acknowledged in any way. Even children learned this at an early age. Even husbands and wives did not talk about what went on anywhere but in the open areas between the tepees and outside of the village during hunts, forages, etc, involving groups. If he and Summer Swan had been seen by the river, making love, their privacy was insured, even there. All sexual activity by couples was their business only, even in the hot summer nights when many slept outside in front of their homes.

Tall Tree did wish that Soaring Eagle had seen him with Summer Swan. He knew he loved her already, but had little choice but to wait for her to come to him. The question was, would she ever come to him?

* * * *

Summer Swan walked toward Tall Tree in the cool morning, her breath making small clouds as she breathed. The warmth of the day before was not to return now until the new grass sprouted and the trees produced new leaves.

She smiled at him and moved to the large cooking circle where she put meat, which she had taken from the storage tepee to the pot hanging over the smoldering fire. The pot was perfect for soup or stew. It was the stomach of a buffalo, hung on sticks. Red-hot stones scooped from the fire circle dropped into it heated the soup. She stoked the fire and added fresh wood. From her pocket, she took herbs that she added to the meat. Later she would dig some more wild onions, turnips, and other roots from the prairie to enhance her stew.

Other women came one or two at a time and put meat wrapped in leaves in the hot ashes to bake. Their food was plentiful, but bland. Plentiful was the important thing. A fresh deer or rabbit, even a fox or big cat would bring variety to them all through the cold times.

* * * *

Soaring Eagle with toddling twins, one on each side, holding his hand, walked to the fire and greeted those there. The boys saw Summer Swan. They dropped their father's hands and scurried toward her on robust hands and knees. She laughed as she sat on the ground with them crawling all over her. She loved them, Soaring Eagle thought as he watched. Her cheeks were flushed. Was it the cold air, or the time she spent with Tall Tree? It was none of his business, but he could not help wondering. Had she had that glow the morning after they made love? He did not know, because like a fool, he stayed away from her the next day.

* * * *

When the twins spied Little Crane, they scurried to meet her as she came from her home. Her face was stern from her father's lecture, at least until she saw the boys. A grin replaced her frown and she raced to them. Well, if she was not to have a new mother, at least she still had her twins, knowing that they loved her as much as she loved them.

* * * *

Two mornings later, Summer Swan awoke feeling ill. What had she eaten last night? She raced from her tepee onto the prairie behind her tepee. As she emptied her stomach, she knew, just as she had the first time. She was pregnant. Pregnant with Soaring Eagle's child. Tall Tree had been too recent. By the Gods, what was she to do? She knew Tall Tree would marry her with another man's babe in her stomach, but that was not right. Moreover, Soaring Eagle did not want her. She returned to her home and returned to her sleeping robes, where she allowed the first falling tears of the many that would come within the next few mornings. She wished she had more knowledge of medicine so she could end the problem. She signed deeply, knowing she could never do that. A babe, no matter the father, is the most important thing in the world.

Little Crane missed her at the cooking fire and came, tapping on her door. "Summer Swan, can I come in?"

"Yes." The child looked surprised to find the woman still abed. "Do not look like that, Child. I am a bit ill, probably from something I ate. Later today, I will go out and find some herbs for an upset stomach. Would you like to help me? We should pick as many herbs and roots as we can find in case others become sick, too. Ask your father for permission and we will go when the sun is high."

* * * *

Tall Tree granted permission, only half listening to his daughter, until he realized the ill person was Summer Swan herself. He carefully questioned Little Crane, not wanting to implant any ideas into her already over-active brain.

An hour before the two females planned to leave, he took his bow and quiver and headed out in search of small game. This would give him an excuse to come across them accidentally, away from camp.

And it happened just as he planned, except he had to wait for them. His hunt was so successful that he even had time to dress and skin the three rabbits, the small fox, and the tortoise he killed.

He saw Summer Swan moving gracefully, head down as she searched the ground for whatever she sought, it did not matter to him. All that mattered was that he would get a chance to talk to her. Little Crane ran ahead, shouting to the woman whenever she thought she found something. He knew his daughter would tire of this escapade long before Summer Swan had finished, so he would suggest she return to the village with his dead creatures while he hunted for more.

"Look, there is father. He carries a full string. I wonder what he killed. Hello, father," she called to him.

"Hello, Little Crane. Come see what your great hunter brought for the fire tonight. Hello, Summer Swan. Are you having any success in your hunt?"

She smiled and nodded. "It is easier now to find what I seek now that the tall grasses are dying back and the soil is easy to dig. Later when the ground is frozen, it will be much harder, so I want to get as many things as I can while they are available. We will have many illnesses, sore throats and achy bones before the ground softens again."

Idle talk continued until, as he planned, Little Crane tired of the hunt. He suggested she return to the village with his kills and soon she was but a running dot outside the camp. "Summer Swan, you are so beautiful. Can I kiss you?" She smiled and nodded. He took her bag from her and dropped it to the ground beside his weapons.

The kiss was long and deep, but not as deep as he desired. She felt his cock press against her as his hand moved to her breast. She moved slightly away, forcing him to drop his hand. She looked at him before asking, "Would you like to come to my tepee tonight? Come after Little Crane is asleep. I will be waiting." With that, she turned to continue her search for medicines.

Chapter 18

Summer Swan was the only thing on Tall Tree's mind all day. The hours seemed to crawl slower than a snail. To keep himself busy, he continued to hunt small game. He moved toward the river and saw Soaring Eagle doing the same. He hailed his friend, his competition. They sat together on the riverbank, stabbing arrows into the water like young boys, laughing as they caught an occasional fish. This was as close as the two friends had been since childhood and it felt right.

Finally Soaring Eagle spoke. "My friend, I must ask how you feel about Summer Swan."

Tall Tree kept his gaze on the water, trying to think of a way to answer. "She is a beautiful woman."

Soaring Eagle laughed. "Yes, she is. And a good mother to my sons."

"Yes, and to my daughter, Little Crane."

"She made me a heavy buffalo robe for the cold times."

"And she made one for me, as well. And one for Little Crane."

"Also for the twins."

The two men were silent for a long while, each realizing they were getting nowhere with this discussion. They returned to stabbing fish and talked of hunting together the next day, hopefully for a deer or two. They walked back to the village, carrying their fish, and agreed to meet again in the morning. If Tall Tree thought the day was long, the evening hours were worse. After they ate, he sent a pouting Little Crane to bed. He sat with the other braves around the fire, talking of days past and hunts to come. Summer Swan had disappeared quite some time before and he was anxious to sneak off to her tepee. He stretched as if tired, nodded to those nearby, and walked slowly to his home. Little Crane was still awake and began chattering as soon as he went inside.

He chided her for being awake still, but that did no good. She quieted but lay with her eyes squeezed so tight, he laughed. "Ok, Little One, I will tell you a story. What do you want to hear?" Immediately he realized his mistake. He should never have given her a choice. She would want to hear about her mother and this night, of all nights, he hid not want his dead wife in his head.

"Tell me about my mama."

"I have told you a million times. Let me tell you about your grandmother, my mother."

"You always tell me not to exaggerate. You have not told me a million times about anything. Ok, you can tell me about my grandmother."

"She died of a fever before you were born. I was a young man still learning to be a hunter and a warrior. She was tall and very beautiful."

"As beautiful as Summer Swan?"

"Hush. You are supposed to listen and ask your questions tomorrow. Now, no more talking.

"She was tall and had braids that ended on top of her head. They were so long that she sat on them if she did not wind them around her head. As a child, I loved it when she took her hair down and bushed it with a hard bristled tool my father made her for just that purpose. Sometimes, when they thought I was asleep, he would brush her hair until it was untangled and flowed freely around her shoulders and down her back."

What he did not tell his daughter was that his father would bury his face in her long hair and pull it aside so he could kiss her shoulders. He would lift the hair up and bury his face under it as he rubbed her breasts, out of sight from prying young eyes. She would make little gasping sounds and giggles, too. They would lie together, whispering and moving beside a pile of sleeping robes they piled between them and his view. He could hear their bodies as they moved. His mother made low moans and his father breathed hard until he growled deeply in throat. They might talk again for a while, or they might not. He would fall asleep and be unaware that their time, doing whatever they were doing, was longer and there was more moaning. His mother would whimper even and cry out for more, more of whatever it was. Later when he learned, he was glad for them both. Their mating was full of love, unlike his own with Little Crane's mother. Dewdrops was a pleasant woman who did all wifely things perfectly except one, she did not like the sex part of marriage no matter what he did nor how hard he tried to please her. She would smile and say, "Do not worry, husband. It is not important." However, it was important to Tall Tree.

"Your grandmother, my mother, never raised her voice or hand to me or the other children. A look from her was enough to cause pain in the heart of anyone who she cast her eyes upon. Once I threw a rock that hit another child, causing blood to run. My mother came to see what the crying was about. She pointed to our tepee and gave me that *look*. I would have to tell my father what I had done. She would not tell him. I would have to do it and all the time I waited for him to return home, I pondered my punishment. Sometime it would be a whipping with a thick branch from a cottonwood tree, one I had to pick myself. Sometimes it was that I had to stay in our tepee for days, all by myself. Sometimes I got no meals or had stand outside while it stormed. But always, I had to apologize to the one I had harmed. That was the worst part of punishment."

Little Crane was still and breathing the soft cadence of sleep. He covered her and stoked the heating fire. He slid off his clothing and wrapped himself in the long buffalo cloak Summer Swan made for him. Just thoughts of her were enough to make his penis stiffen, even the cold that greeted him outside did no soften it.

He moved slowly and quietly, staying in the shadows as much as possible. His instincts told him he that eyes followed him, but he did not care. All he wanted was to be in the arms and body of the woman who waited for him.

* * * *

Summer Swan was waiting. She had washed her body from the bucket she got from the river the day before. In the water, she added crushed petals of wild flowers picked during the hot time and saved. They gave off sweet aromas that filled her home and covered her body. She heard his soft knock and untied the straps holding the door closed.

Tall Tree stepped inside and turned to retie the door before looking at her. His breath became a soft moan as he looked at her naked body in the flickering firelight. He dropped his robe, showing his naked body with its enormous cock, sticking straight out at her. She dropped to her knees in front of him and teased the end of it with her tongue. He jutted forward with his hips, trying to push the erection into her mouth. She laughed softly, but continued to tease him now with her tongue and lips that tightened around the tip. Again, he moaned and his hips began a motion of mating, wanting more than she was giving him.

When he thought he could not stand the teasing another second, she took all of him into her mouth, even into her upper throat. Her tongue circled his hardness and she sucked him in and out. She squeezed his balls, gently, and ran her fingers into his butt crack, rubbing his anus. She inserted a finger inside him, every so gently. His moan, was it pleasure or pain? Whatever it was, it was enough to cause him to release. His semen ran down her chin onto her breasts and down her stomach.

She quickly lay on her back and rubbed his seed over her breasts. He knelt beside her and began to lick it. His mouth and tongue found every drop. They worked their way from her lips, down her chin, all around her breasts, taking special care of her nipples until they hardened into tiny points, across the length of her stomach until he reached her pussy, wet with her own excitement. He dipped his tongue into her, licking her sweetness, but feeling it return as fast as he removed it. His fingers delved into the depths of her womanhood. She was moving to meet his movements inside her. When his mouth found her swollen clit, she lifted her hips to meet him. He sucked on the hardness of her center until she cried out. She whimpered and held his head against her as her hips bounced. Her hips finally dropped to the sleeping robe, but Tall Tree continued to lick her wetness away before he stopped.

Never had he felt the power of a woman, a woman who gave as much as she got. He already desired her again, but forced himself to remain calm. Instead of trying to mount her, he wrapped his arms around her, holding her close. She snuggled tightly against him, burying her face in his shoulder. He waited for her to say something, anything, but she remained quiet. After a few minutes, she began to kiss him tiny kisses without moving her face. The kisses were one of the most exciting things he had ever felt. When she stopped, he felt disappointment before he realized she was asleep.

He held her without moving. He wanted to hold her like this forever. But if tonight was all he was to have of her, he would relish it forever. Soon he slept, too.

Chapter 19

Soaring Eagle watched as Tall Tree entered the home of Summer Swan. He knew they would spend the night in one another's arms, doing the things he and she once did in his tepee. How could he have been so stupid? He presumed, wrongly, that she would stay with him forever, caring for his sons, and sharing his bed when he wanted her. His mistake was telling Little Crane that he would never marry again. And telling her where Summer Swan could hear.

He was fond of Summer Swan and she had been incredible in his bed. Never would he have hurt her intentionally, but thoughtlessly, he had hurt her and hurt her badly. She was a strong woman with a mind of her own. She refused to be a plaything, which was how he viewed her. Until, that is, she found someone else to take to her bed. He was sure that Tall Tree loved the woman and now he realized that he loved her, too. Not the way he loved She Who Smiles, but in a different way as the two women were so different. Now, what chance did he have?

The two men hunted together in the morning as agreed. Their companionship was real and strong as it had always been. Tall Tree was in high spirits with his newfound desire, as Soaring Eagle was dismayed at his loss of that same desire. They killed four deer that day before returning to camp. Their success was cause for a celebration. The men gutted and dressed the deer and gave the skins to the women to start the tanning process. They played games like children. There was much laughter and enjoyment until the worst happened.

In a knife-throwing contest, one of the young braves lost his balance as he released his blade at the target. The wild throw landed in the lower shoulder of Soaring Eagle, right above his heart. People began yelling and screaming like a pack of scared buffalo. Only Tall Tree and Summer Swan ran to the downed man. He pulled the knife from Soaring Eagle and she staunched the blood flow with a piece of deerskin she cut from her skirt.

She cut off the shirt covering his wound and winced to see the depth of the cut. She ordered water and it appeared almost immediately. Little Crane was by her side instantly. "Go, child, to my tepee and bring my bag of medicines. Someone find some more soft cloths, lots of them. Clean ones, too. Nothing dirty. Hurry. He is losing much blood. Oh, by the Gods, Soaring Eagle, I will not let you die." There were tears in her eyes that she raised her face to the sky as if praying.

* * * *

In that moment, Tall Tree knew. He knew whom Summer Swan loved. He had suspected it, but now he was certain. His heart felt empty as he watched her cleanse the wound of his friend, his competition, and his victor. She dipped cloths in the water over and over again, until she was sure the cut was clean inside. She sprinkled powders that she took from her bag onto one of the wet cloths and held it inside the cut, stopping the bleeding. She held it in place with her one hand while she wiped the face of Soaring Eagle with a wet cloth, letting water dripping into his open lips.

He coughed and opened his eyes. Confused and in pain, he tried to sit up only to find Summer Swan and Tall Tree holding him down. "What happened? Let me up."

"A knife hit you. And if you want to stand up, then just go ahead and do it. Without help, of course." Summer Swan moved back and watched with no emotion as Soaring Eagle tried to sit. He fell back.

"Now, we will put you on a travois and take you to your tepee and you will rest. Do you understand?" She was firm. "Where are the boys?"

"They are with Sweet Flower. We will get her travois." Someone answered and within a few second, a warrior laid the travois beside the prone man.

"Carefully, four of you, lift him on to the travois. I will support under his back so he does not bend." They instantly obeyed Summer Swan's orders. Soaring Eagle moaned slightly before he clamped his teeth together to stop his weakness from escaping. Inside his home, they repeated the process, laying him on his sleeping robes. This time he was silent.

Tall Tree sat cross-legged beside his friend. "Does this mean we do not go hunting tomorrow?" he asked.

Soaring Eagle grinned. "Yes, let us plan it. You will have to tie me on my horse, I think. Maybe we can figure out how to build a giant pack for me to sit in, like a big papoose." Both men laughed.

"Tell me, Tall Tree, how did this happen? I remember young He Who Yawns getting ready to throw his knife, then nothing."

Summer Swan's voice was hard. "Maybe he stumbled, maybe he yawned. It does not matter now, because his blade hit you rather than the target. Now, I will give you something to make you sleep. I will stay this night if you need anything." She held a cup she prepared to his lips and forced the liquid between over his teeth.

"Yow. That tasted worse than skunk juice. What is this foul thing are you feeding me?"

"It does not matter. Just drink it. *Now!*" He swallowed what she gave him, scowling. He lay back, feeling weak and tired.

* * * *

Tall Tree hated the idea of her staying with the wounded man, but he also felt guilty. Someone had to help him and who better than a medicine woman? "I will leave you now. There is a young brave I need to see."

Soaring Eagle heard him and said in a haze, "Do not hurt him. He did not mean it. His guilt will be punishment enough. Promise, my friend?"

"If that is your wish, then so it will be. Goodnight. I will come in the morning." He nodded at the woman and left. He went in search of He Who Yawns, but could not find him. He would find him in the morning, he was sure.

* * * *

Find him, he did. The young man, barely more than a child, had left the village. He found an anthill not far away. There he sat, naked, as he cut himself with the knife Summer Swan had pulled from the chief. With each cut, he asked the gods for forgiveness. The blood drew the ants, as he knew it would. Some they were swarming all over his body, biting in each cut. He continued to slice his legs and arms, then his face and hands. Tears ran down his face, but he made not a sound. Lastly, he cut off his penis, bringing a howl of pain from his throat. He fell back and let the creatures consume him, one tiny bite at a time, tiny painful bites. He did not see it as an accident, but a crime for which nature would extract the ultimate punishment.

Chapter 20

The days passed quickly. Summer Swan rose early, leaving the tepee to relieve herself and to vomit as she did every morning. She tried to remember how long this lasted when she was pregnant with her dead little girl, but could not. She could find no herbs to alleviate this morning malady, so she suffered as many women did. No one was the wiser except for Little Crane who wandered around the village after her morning 'necessity.'

"Summer Swan, why are you throwing up? Are you sick? What can I do to help?"

"It is nothing. Something I ate, probably."

"That is what you said the other times, too. Should I get someone to help you?"

"No, Child. Tell no one. It is nothing and it will pass soon. Now, it is too cold for you to be wandering around outside. Go home and warm up. Later we will get the twins from Sweet Flower and take them to see their father. He can sit up now and is complaining all the time about having to stay inside. One more night, I think, and then I can go home."

* * * *

Little Crane, like any other 6 year old, was unable to keep a secret. Back in their tepee, she curled up in her robes and waited patiently for Tall Tree to awaken. He stretched finally and sat up. "Father, did you know that Summer Swan is sick?"

"No, I did not. What is wrong with her?" He felt an instant concern and had to force himself to remain calm.

"I do not know. But every time I see her in the morning outside, she throws up. She says it is nothing and will go away soon, but I am worried about her."

Tall Tree took a deep breath. He had no doubt what it was, but could not tell his young child. "I think she is right and we do not have anything to worry about. I will talk to her today."

"No, do not tell her. I am not supposed to talk about it. She would be angry with me if she knew I told you. Please!"

He smiled and pulled the child onto his lap, "I promise no one will ever know where I heard about her illness. So instead of worrying, why not laugh?" He began to tickle her and her worry disappeared. He loved to hear her giggles, he loved her more than life.

*   *   *   *

Sweet Flower recovered slowly, day by day. Summer Swan told her that she probably would never have children of her own because of the torture the renegades had inflicted, but Sweet Flower was glad to be alive. The accident with the knife hurt more than Soaring Eagle.

Sweet Flower and He Who Yawns had plans to marry when she was well enough. Her heart was not broken, not really, because she knew she did not love the young warrior. He was pleasant and understanding and desired her as she was. No other man would want her, looking the way she did. She cried as he went to meet the gods and settled back to the life she had. Taking care of other children was her reward, as she adored every child, especially the twins.

Little Crane came for them early to take them to see their father. Sweet Flower watched as the little boys dressed themselves, laughing along with them at their follies. When they were ready to go, they ran to her, showering her with kisses and hugs. Those gestures would give her great pleasure all day until their return later. She dreaded the day when they would go back to their father permanently, but she pushed that aside and she began her daily exercises, which were not as much fun without the boisterous duo exercising with her.

* * * *

The boys were walking, or rather, running now. Soaring Eagle and Summer Swan could hear them laughing before they reached the tepee flap and that brought a smile to both pairs of lips. The twins rushed inside like a pair of rolling little bears as they hit his midsection knocking him backward. Summer Swan laughed with them then left quietly to help with the never-ending chores of the women. They did not notice her leave.

She spent part of her afternoon in her own tepee. She napped and daydreamed of the child in her stomach. She wanted a daughter to replace the babe she lost, but a son was no less desirable. It was dusk when she returned to the twins and Soaring Eagle. Even Little Crane was exhausted and asked, "How does Sweet Flower manage these two when she can hardly stand? Land Hunter pulled my hair so hard that I am going to be bald forever. And Iron Eyes hit uncle so hard that he has a black eye. Now that you are back, I am going home. Do you want me to take the brats to Sweet Flower on my way to eat?"

Summer Swan laughed. "No, perhaps they should stay here tonight. We shall see. Anyway, it is time to take them to eat and get new packing for their night clothing." She changed them, one at a time while Soaring Eagle held the other to keep him from 'helping.'

"I will bring you some food when we come back. We will not be long."

It was obvious to Summer Swan that Soaring Eagle felt a sense of dismay at her suggestion that the boys stay with them tonight. The look on his face told it all. He yawned loudly. "I am so tired. These two are more than a sick man can handle. Perhaps it would be better if they stay a night or two more with Sweet Flower. By then I should be back on my feet and able to handle them by myself." He slid down in his sleeping robe and turned away. Summer Swan had no time to think this through as two running babes were already out the door and almost to the fires.

Once she and the twins had eaten, they returned to Soaring Eagle's tepee. She peeked inside before letting the boys in. She could see their father asleep in his robes. One arm and one naked leg were uncovered. He was apparently as tired as he said he was. All right, she thought, one more night with Sweet Flower for the boys.

Sweet Flower was delighted to see them. Summer Swan helped her ready them for bed, wondering aloud how the crippled woman managed. "It really is not that hard. I suggest to them that a race to see who could be quietest in their robes would give the winner a special treat in the morning. Within less that the time it takes for me to teeter over to them, they are both asleep. In the morning, I declare a tie or say I fell asleep before they did. Whatever, they never question me."

They two women sat watching the fire. Summer Swan pondered how to approach the death of Sweet Flower's husband to be, but before she could ask, the younger woman began to speak. "He Who Yawns should not have died. He did nothing intentional, but he was far too honorable. He did not even wait to see the result of his error before he decided he must pay. Tall Tree said Soaring Eagle did not want him hurt for his poor aim. His death was his own decision and I cry to think how much pain he suffered before he died. I liked him very much and we would have been happy together, I think. He knew I could not have children and he said he cared only for me and not what could not be." She hung her head and her voice lowered. "He came to my bed twice and it was wonderful. I was afraid because of what those men did to me, but He Who Yawns was gentle and soon I was feeling the things other women experience. I did not know that a penis could feel so good or that lips down there could bring heaven to me. For those two nights, I will always be thankful, as no other man would want someone like me."

Summer Swan hugged Sweet Flower. "That is not necessarily the case. I bet you never expected to have He Who Yawns to pursue you and ask you to marry. So why cannot some other warrior want you the same? You are a beautiful woman with the sweetest face in the world. If I were a man, I think I would pursue you." They both laughed.

"Thank you. The babies are asleep and you must go see your patient. Perhaps we can talk again." They said their goodnights and Summer Swan returned to Soaring Eagle's home.

Chapter 21

Summer Swan had an idea. It was the perfect solution. She would try to get Soaring Eagle and Sweet Flower together. Even as her thoughts began to dwell on her new plan, she felt a strange hollowness in her stomach. She stopped outside the tepee and sat on a tree stump. Whom was she kidding? The only one she wanted with Soaring Eagle was she. The idea of him on top of any other woman made her nauseous. Well, she would see to his wound and return this night to her home. Being near him, every night, across the warming fire from him, was more than she wanted to experience again.

He was asleep as she knelt to lift the dressing she had tied around his chest, covering the wound. In an instant, he was sitting and she was in his arms. His lips found her and his tongue circled inside her mouth. She felt a fever rising in her, one she did not want to stop. She knew she should stop this, but felt the wetness already in her vagina. She moaned as one hand lifted her shirt and began rubbing her breasts, first one, and then the other. His mouth and tongue would not release her. His fingers began to pinch her nipples, causing them to harden.

He used both hands to pull off her clothes. Before she could move away, he pressed her back onto his robes. His mouth worshipped her breasts as his hands moved lower and lower until one began squeezing her ass cheeks and the other claimed her clit. The second he touched her there, she knew she was his and begged him not to stop. He chuckled to himself as if he would or could stop.

Her cries built higher and stronger until he thought she might explode into tiny pieces, and hoped she would. She dropped her hips back down and pulled at his penis until he knelt between her spread legs. He teased her by moving it in a scant distance, then pulling it back out. She dug her fingernails into his ass and bounced her pussy up against his groin. His desire ignited at her movements until he was as deep in her as possible. Together they moved, each of them trying to please the other as only a man and woman in throes of passion until they reached the ultimate satisfaction. They slept.

* * * *

Soaring Eagle awoke with a start and realized the woman was gone. Her clothes were gone as well. He started to rise, and then lay back down. Why had she left him after such wonderful sex? Had he done something wrong? His penis that was hard on awakening now began to shrink back down. He could smell her on his hands, arms, and sleeping robes. It was a smell he wanted to inhale forever and now she was gone.

He lay back on his robes, letting his mind wander. He knew she has spent nights with Tall Tree and for the first time, admitted to himself he was jealous. She was her own woman, of that there was no doubt, but he wanted her to be *his* woman, and *his alone*. He also knew his own big mouth had given her reason to distrust him and that for her to marry him was out of the question. He had to figure some way to undo the damage he had done.

* * * *

In her tepee, Summer Swan dropped to her sleeping robe and covered her face with her hands as the tears fell. She could smell him on her hands and body. She cursed herself for giving in to his lust, and even more for giving in to her own. He knew he did not love her or want her for a wife. She heard him say so himself.

She forced herself to stand and left her home, naked and barefoot in the snow to go for a water bag. She stood outside in the freezing mist and poured the liquid over her body, from the head to the ground. She rubbed herself with the near frozen water, washing away every scent and body fluid on her body. She ran back into her tepee, threw some buffalo chips on the heating fire, and rolled up in her robes before crying herself to sleep.

Chapter 22

Shouts woke her. Sounds of fighting followed. She jumped up, pulled on her clothing, and grabbed a buffalo skin coat before she opened the flap enough to peak out. Her eyes widened as she saw strange men running around the village. She took her long knife from the box on the floor and secreted it inside her skirt at the waist. She stepped outside her tepee and stood quietly until she saw a man entered Sweet Flower's home.

She ran across the village. A pair of fighting men blocked her from passing. It was Tall Tree and an enemy. Without missing a pace, she pulled her knife and stabbed the war painted man in his back, just as he was about to use his tomahawk on Tall Tree.

She ran until she was in Sweet Flower's tepee. A man leaned over Sweet Flower, pulling back her clothes. Again, Summer Swan did not hesitate. She stabbed him as she had the first man, pulling him backward so he would not fall on her or the babies beside the prone woman. The flap moved and another man stepped inside. Soaring Eagle, checking his sons. He saw the dead warrior, nodded to them, and disappeared outside.

The flap moved again, but this time both women smiled. Little Crane ran straight into her arms, crying just as the twins were. "Shhhhh, little ones. We will be fine. I will not let anything happen to you." In her heart, she knew she had been lucky so far, that she was no match for a warring warrior, but she would die trying to protect them all.

Sweet Flower's voice, barely heard, was quivering as she asked, "Who are these men? What do they want?"

"I do not know. A raid is all I can tell you. Who or why, I have no idea." She lay Little Crane in Sweet Flower's arms and pulled the twins close to her, one on each side of her body. She would have held them on her lap, but needed to keep herself unburdened in case she had to defend them again.

The sounds of the fighting diminished slowly. Tall Tree opened the flap and announced it was safe for Summer Swan to come out, but the children should stay inside. He did not want them to see the bodies, the blood and gore of the dead. Only one of their tribe was dead. Man of Horses had an arrow through his throat. Summer Swan ran to him and held his head in her lap. Her tears slid down her cheeks and formed rivulets in the deep wrinkles of the old man she had grown to love as a father.

She did not move as the men gather up the enemy dead. They tied the bodies to the backs of the horses on which they had ridden to the village before they attacked if anyone could tell them from whence they came. Otherwise, as enemies, they would become food for the creatures of the Plains, unworthy as warriors sent off to the gods.

Two were still alive, at least as she watched them refusing to answer questions. She shook her head, knowing that their silence would only resort in intense pain until they pleaded for death.

Her normally soft nature had hardened to steel with the death of the man in her lap. She wanted to see the enemy suffer. She wanted to hurt them herself, so she gently moved the head of Man of Horses to the ground and walked over to see the two captives close up. One was on a fallen log, a log the children pretended was a horse they could ride. The other dangled from a branch of a dead tree, swinging gently back and forth, as he watched the activity around him.

Without a word, she pulled her knife from her skirt pocket and carefully, cut away his loincloth to free his manhood. She lifted the point to his thighs and made a series of cuts from his knee to his groin, first on one leg and then the other. "Why are you here? Why did you kill my father? Who are you? Speak or my knife will remove your manhood next."

He clamped his mouth shut. She raised her knife again and quickly cut off one of his balls. He screamed in pain. "Talk! I will remove the other one next." Still he refused to answer. Summer Swan took her time cutting the second ball. Blood ran down his legs and squirted to the ground. "Are you ready to die? You will bleed to death from where your cock is shriveled up inside you if you do not talk." Again, he refused to answer. Summer Swan looked up into his eyes and slowly shook her head. "Is it worth dying for? Will the gods reward you for this? I think they will not. This is your last chance." She tugged on his penis until she pulled it as far to its length as she could. The knife was poised and ready. The man closed his eyes and Summer Swan cut off his penis.

Soaring Eagle reached around her to take the knife from her hand. Her head dropped and tears soaked her shirt. She turned and walked quietly back to sit and hold the head of the dead man she loved. She chanted quietly, eyes closed, face toward the heavens.

Tall Tree and Soaring Eagle stood together a few feet from the hanging man. His blood stained the ground as his heart pumped his life away. Other villagers stood in small groups, whispering to themselves. Never had they seen Summer Swan as a vindictive, cruel person.

* * * *

Soaring Eagle spoke to the man tied to the downed tree trunk. "Do you wish to die as your friend did? Think about it this night. Tomorrow we can let you return home or have you die a painful death. It is your decision."

Tall Tree turned to those standing behind him. "The man was a fool. He let his life flow away because of his stubbornness. Had he answered, he might have lived. Summer Swan felt the need for revenge against those who killed Man of Horses and terrorized our village. His was a sad waste of life, his own waste of life. It is the right of any person to kill an enemy for what he did or had done. All should know that she also killed an enemy who was attacking me and she stopped another who tried to rape Sweet Flower and harm our children. She is a woman like no other. She is our shaman, our Mother, and we are blessed to have her."

The crowd clapped, cheered, and yelled in agreement. Summer Swan did not respond to the tribute. It was as if she did not hear it. She was lost in her own mind where she conversed to Man of Horses and listened to his words. She nodded that she understood and let the men take the body from her arms before she went to own tepee.

Chapter 23

The people of the tribe prepared for the burial of Man of Horses, giving him up to the gods. A platform placed far away from the village, but within sight of the people. Both men and women in warm clothing rode to the wooded area along the river to cut sturdy tree limbs and trunks. They dragged them back and tied them together with buffalo sinew. Once the structure was erect, they affixed a community ladder to the side for the body to be lifted to the platform surface made of buffalo skins.

They dressed his body in his best buckskin clothing and wrapped it tightly inside his sleeping robes with the fur side against him to keep him warm on his trip. His weapons lay beside him and jars and bags of food and his belongings were next to him. Man of Horses now could go to his gods, the long journey of a good man.

Once Man of Horses reclined on his last earthly bed, the tribe gathered around it. They played drums and musical instruments they had created. Many danced and chanted. Summer Swan sat in her tepee alone and prayed for him and a quick journey. Little Crane tapped gently on the flap before sticking her head through it.

"Summer Swan, my father says it is time for you to come."

"Tell him I am not coming. They can celebrate without me. I have no wish to join them."

The child left. There was another knock on the flap and she said, "Go away, Little Crane. Leave me alone this night."

It was not Little Crane. The shadow that filled the floor around her was from a tall man. Without turning, she knew it was Soaring Eagle. She knew his odors and the sound of his footsteps. He sat cross-legged beside her in one graceful movement. "Summer Swan, why do you say you will not come to us. You are our Mother, our Shaman. It is your responsibility to lead us in these rites."

She turned on him angrily. "Who said I wanted to be the Mother or Shaman. I never asked for the responsibilities and I do not want them. You go away, too. Leave me to grieve alone. Respect my pain and privacy, as I respect yours. Now go!"

Instead of leaving, he stood and lifted her up until she stood before him. "It is the will of the gods that you are the Mother and Shaman. And the will of the Chief." He pulled her to him and gently kissed her tear-swollen eyes and wiped the wetness from her cheeks. His lips touched hers gently. His arms pulled her close, but only to put her head on his shoulder. "You will come, now." He led her outside into the twilight of the day, declared by the gods to be when a person left earth to meet them.

He held her hand while they walked to the platform. The crowd quieted, awaiting her and her words. As they stood together, the last rays of the sun pushed through the clouds to shine directly on them. To some it meant the gods placed them together forever, but to Tall Tree it was a sunray of pain. Summer Swan failed to notice him at all. Soaring Eagle took it as a sign that overwhelmed him.

Finally, Summer Swan raised her arms toward the heavens. "We send our beloved father to you this night. Savages who invaded our home murdered Man of Horses. We thank you for saving all others, but we grieve for his loss. In my heart, I am angry with you for allowing this to happen. I would have gladly given my life for his a hundred times over."

Surprised murmurs swept through the crowd. No one ever showed anger to the gods. It was unthinkable. Many feared anger they were positive the gods would turn on them.

"Look down at me, not those around me, nor the man who gave his life today. I and I alone who feel this fury at what you have done in taking this wonderful man. Oh, yes, you probably think because he was old, his life was over. For me, it was just beginning. Never before did I have a man who loved me as my father did when I was a child. He loved me as a daughter and taught me many things a father would have. Now you have taken him. What have you left me now? I am selfish, yes. I would rather join him right now on the platform than continue on this earth without him to guide me."

She moved through the crowd to the foot of the ladder and started a slow climb upward when a tremendous wind ripped across the prairie. The wind tore the ladder loose from its bindings and dropped to the ground gently, as if to protect Summer Swan from harm. When she arose, she looked skyward and then at the body above. She stepped away and began chanting a farewell prayer. Soon all were chanting with her. The clouds opened and a beautiful full moon lightened the prairie. A coyote howled and a herd of wild horses ran the crest of a far away hill, silhouetted against the starlit sky.

Man of Horses was on his way to his gods.

Chapter 24

The night seemed to have changed into something magical. The air seemed to warm and smiles were on every face. Around the campfire they sat and talked, laughed and teased, and snuggled and crept away to their tepees. It was as if the gods were pleased with them and they were pleased because of it.

Even Summer Swan ate with a new appetite. She giggled at the twin's antics before seriousness swept her face. Walking toward them was Sweet Flower, aided by Little Crane. It was a miracle from the gods! Everyone stood and crowded around the two, exclaiming their delight. Only Summer Swan was not surprised. She knew how hard the crippled woman had been trying to walk. Perhaps the leg rubs with prairie roots and herbs had helped, but perhaps not.

Now that Sweet Flower had achieved this much, Summer Swan knew that nothing would stop Sweet Flower from being a whole woman again. Except, thought Summer Swan, for the young woman's inability to have a child. Little Crane led Sweet Flower to where Summer Swan sat and helped her take her place on the ground. The three huddled tightly together and enjoyed the happiness of the occasion.

The men danced around the fire circle until exhausted. Couples found one another and crept off into the darkness. Tired children were herded away by the young women to join Sweet Flower in her tepee or their own, if they had no mate.

She moved away from the fire to sit between Tall Tree and Soaring Eagle who lounged apart from the group, near the dangling body of the man she had killed. She looked at the body with no regrets, only sadness that he preferred death to honesty. She did not consider that he died to protect his tribe. His reason was unimportant to her, and if she had to do it over again, she would have no qualms.

"There is something I would like to share with you two, if it is alright." They both nodded. "When I killed that man, something seemed to happen to me. It was a sense of power and lust and pain and fear, all at once. For the first time I think that I understand some of men's emotions. Like the strength and hot blood after a successful hunt or the besting of enemies in a fight. Is it the blood you spill that urges your desires? Is it because nearing death, you feel the need to further life? Is that the reason men are so horny at those times?"

Soaring Eagle nodded slowly. "Yes, perhaps there is some truth in what you ask. I remember wanting to bed She Who Smiles the minute I returned to camp. It was always incredible with her then. She understood and met me with as much passion as I had for her."

Tall Tree nodded. "My wife was not like yours, Soaring Eagle. She was a sweet person with no physical desires of any kind. She tolerated my lust those times, but did not respond as I wished she would. I knew other men and their wives joined repeatedly after a battle, or even a hunt. After she died, the women who bedded with me were nice, but it was not like the couples that loved one another. I have wondered if the fault was mine."

Summer Swan took his hand. "It was not your fault. You are a wonderful lover, Tall Tree. I know you had deep feelings for her, but the problem was hers, not yours." She leaned up to kiss his cheek. Soaring Eagle felt a pang of jealousy, even though he knew he had driven her to the bed of his friend.

They were quiet for several minutes. Summer Swan finally lifted her head, carefully looking first one then the other directly in their eyes. "The blood of the man behind us, I think it made me feel the same way. Something Man of Horses told me one time was that I must be careful not to turn good friends into enemies by preferring one over the other. So, this night, I want to take his advice. I would like you both to join me in my tepee, on my sleeping robes. I want you equally, and have no desire to choose. Will you share me with each other? I am excited sitting here, just thinking about your naked bodies and the things we can do together."

The men arose at the same time, as if rehearsed. In their minds, the men felt emotions of jealousy and planned to be better at satisfying her than his friend. Each took one of her hands and the three of them moved away from the dying fire toward her tepee next to the abandoned one of Man of Horses. She whispered as they neared it. "Tonight he is there, on his robes, smiling as he listens to our lovemaking. Probably wishing he could join us."

Chapter 25

Both men had penises so erect they hurt, but neither had an idea of how to begin. Summer Swan spoke, with a smile. "For two incredible warriors, you seem at a loss as to what to do. I do not remember this ever happening before. In the past, you always seemed to know what you wanted to do. What is so different now?" Neither man answered. "I see. Well, I guess I will have to show you what I want then."

She moved away from them and slowly with her back to them, lifted her dress from the bottom up. The air temperature in the tepee was warm, although the fire had died down to embers that glowed enough for the men to see the smooth curved of her ass and long legs. She bent over to pick up the dress, making sure then could see between her thighs.

She held the dress over her front and turned to face them. She let it drop inches at a time until the rise of her breasts and valley between were visible, but not the nipples. "Are you two going to stand there all night or do you expect me to undress you myself?" She laughed and watched them dropping their clothes much as gangling young men with their first woman. Once the clothes hit the ground, they became men again. Her men!

She did not know who pulled the dress from her, but she knew the lips that kissed her breast. Each tit became a place of worship for one of the warriors. With her eyes closed, still she knew which mouth belonged to which man. Each had his own way of kissing and sucking and nibbling on her nipples, which were now hard and pointing out from dark dimpled aureoles.

One breast was cupped and squeezed gently, the other with more power. Both were pleasurable, each in a different way. Neither was better or less than the other was.

Summer Swan lifted her face to kiss first Soaring Eagle, then Tall Tree. Soon a kiss invited the other man to nuzzle and tongue her neck. Her neck was one of her most sensitive spots and she purred her desire each time, even through the kisses.

Her hands found their way to hard, muscular chests. She rubbed each man and found a nipple to squeeze. Sharp intakes of breath told her they liked it. Finally, she moved her hands down stomachs until her fingers found the hair surrounding engorged penises. Careful she did not touch the cocks, she ran her fingers through their hair, knowing it was so exciting that she was not certain how long before one of them pushed his manhood into her hand.

Somehow neither did. They continued to kiss and fondle her breasts until she cupped their balls and squeezed them gently at first, then with more pressure. Tall Tree was first to move her hand to his throbbing member. She took his cue and slid her hand around Soaring Eagle, too. The sounds of their moans excited her even further.

She rubbed their cocks against her stomach and thighs, then across her nether hair. Her hands did not stop their sliding and squeezing of the men. She was in complete control and loving every second. Each time a man's hand tried to reach between her legs, she moved it back up to the tit it was neglecting. Hands there were for later.

She dropped to her knees and rubbed the cocks against her cheeks before taking one in her mouth for a few seconds, then the other. Each time she sucked one, she held it longer than before, enjoying the stabs into her throat. She then replaced it with the other. To slow them down, she encircled each penis around the organ where it left the groin, squeezing enough to slightly dampen ardor. She could feel it was time, which she could not hold them off much longer.

"Are you ready? Do you want to cum? I want to suck you both until you explode." Her words were all it took. She felt the first waves of semen hit her face and in her mouth. The moans, groans, and moving hips made her pussy throb with want, too. She rubbed the cocks against her cheeks, teasing them with her tongue until the dripping stopped. With cum on her face and lips, she kissed each man, pushing him down onto her bed until they lay naked beside one another.

"Do not move, my wonderful men. I will be back in a few minutes. Rest yourselves because the night is just beginning and I want more." She laughed softly and left the tepee, walking to the back of it where she had left bladders of water. She washed her face and body, careful not to touch her wetness between her legs. That was for the men. When she was satisfied that she was clean enough, she returned.

Inside, she stood looking down at them. "I have a pussy full of juice. My body made it while you were enjoying my mouth. Now, I want to enjoy yours." Tall Tree rolled off the blanket and grabbed her around the hips as he rose to his knees. He spread her legs and buried his face in her dripping curls. She began to rock as he sucked her wetness out and rolled her clit with his tongue. She was ready, oh so ready, but not yet. She pulled away.

"I want to lay down now. I want to feel both of your tongues in me. I want you both to taste me. I want you to take turns teasing me. I want you!" Before her shoulders were even on the blanket, her hips lifted and two tongues brushed against one another in their rush to get to her. "Slowly, take turns. Oh, yes, that is perfect. More, more, more." Her hips rose until only her back and shoulders touched the ground. The world exploded in wave after wave of a molten ocean that swept through her groin, up to her tits, and on until her head felt only the pleasures from below.

She dropped exhausted to the blanket. Soaring Eagle moved between her legs again to press his hard cock into her wetness. Tall Trees licked her lips and tits as he watched his friend fucking the beautiful woman they both wanted. His penis was so swollen now that it hurt.

Soaring Eagle pulled out of her just before he exploded. The magnificent hardness of Tall Tree took his place, but his self-control failed him at that point. He came so hard he feared he might hurt her, but her legs wrapped around his hips and she rode with him until he collapsed.

He had barely moved to her side when Soaring Eagle replaced him. The same strong legs encircled his waist and held him inside her until he could wait no longer. His climax was the most exciting he had even experienced. He knew he would share her with his friend whenever she wanted, but she would become his wife. Nothing would stop that, even Tall Tree'

Chapter 26

Just when I think I know human nature, one of them does something that I do not understand. I understand the lust and carnal needs they succumb to. I understand their angers and revenges. I understand their love and protectiveness of their offspring and animals. However, this night, I saw something I will have to ponder. Why would the woman do the thing she did?

The tired threesome slept like a trio of spoons. Tall Tree lay on his side with Summer Swan snuggled against him, breasts hard on his back and her arm around his waist, cupping his penis gently. Soaring Eagle pressed his penis against her butt, enjoying its warmth and his hand over her waist felt her wiry hair where it touched Tall Tree.

In the night, Summer Swan carefully arose, not disturbing the exhausted men, and ran naked outside in the cold night to relieve herself. It was so incredibly cold that her stream gave off steam and a sour odor. She started to enter her home when she saw the unclothed man tied to the log. She did not understand herself even, why she did what she did. Somewhere deep inside her she felt his misery.

She ran into the tepee of Man of Horses and grabbed one of his sleeping robes. She hurried across the center of the village to where the man lay tied. She barely felt his breath and knew he was close to death. Some instinct made her want to rescue him. She wrapped the buffalo robe around him. No, she thought, he is too cold to make any warmth for himself. She carefully lifted on edge of the robe and slid under it, stretching her body over his. She tucked the robe back under him again, and lay with her head on his shoulder. Soon she slept.

The night was starting to fade when she awoke. The warrior was watching her face as she opened his eyes. "Why did you save me?" he asked. Summer Swan just shrugged as she climbed off him and ran back to her tepee.

The men were still asleep, but with their backs to one another. She carefully crawled up between then hoping they would never know she was gone. "What is that?" growled Soaring Eagle as one of her feet accidentally touched him. He sat up and reached to grab her leg that she had tried to keep away from him, only to touch Tall Tree with her other foot. He awakened also and sat up.

"Woman, you are as cold as an icicle. Where have you been?" Tall Tree demanded,

"Well, a woman has needs, you know. My body was full of water. Does that answer your question?"

"Not really," said Soaring Eagle. "To get this cold, you must have been outside a long time."

"Stop picking on me, you two. I am cold! So stop badgering me and warm me up or I will put my cold feet in places you will not like them. See, like this." She pushed one foot into each male lap, wiggling her toes down between their thighs while she giggled quietly at their antics.

Their reactions were just as she had hoped. They forgot the questions and began to warm her. Tall Tree kissed her lips, running his tongue over her teeth and around her mouth. Soaring Eagle moved his hand down to explore her pussy. "I do not believe it. You are even cold inside. Well, I guess it is my job to warm that up." Her clit retracted from the cold the same as her nipples had hardened to tiny point.

Tall Tree warmed her breasts with soft movements and nipple teasing. Soaring Eagle's cock was ready, so he spit on his hard cock to moisten it before gently pushing into her. Her body began to respond and she moved her hips slightly to allow him to penetrate deeper. They both could feel the warm wetness her body was starting to make down in her channel. He increased his rhythm and drew the moisture out. When he could feel the slippery fluid, he lifted his hips enough to put his hand between them. Her tiny button was throbbing throbbed while he rolled it between his fingers. Her movements increased as she met his hand and cock. She stiffened and moaned as her clit sent out an ocean of waves. She pushed his hand away and wrapped her legs around him. They rocked until he came.

Soaring Eagle rolled off her shaking body. Tall Tree immediately replaced his friend. Her vagina was wet with cum, both hers and Soaring Eagle's. Tall Tree found the wetness exciting as he jabbed into her hard. She pulled his shoulders down and kissed him deeply, driving him even further into ecstasy. His climax was so intense that he thought he might have died, but that was all right with him.

She snuggled down between them, kissing their faces and rubbing their chests. She tweaked nipples and teased cocks until she felt awakening between their legs. She withdrew her hands and sat up.

"Enough is enough. It is dawn and you two need to return to your own homes. The children will be awakening soon, and their fathers should be there to feed them. But," she squeezed her nose shut, "clean up first. You smell as if you spent the night fucking. I know your babes and Little Crane are sure to ask." She stood above them, stretching her arms above her head to lift her tits and letting them see every inch of her body before wrapping a blanket around her. "That was pleasant and we should do it again some time."

She smiled as they dressed, both scowling. Her teasing gave them both the idea they were going to get a morning repeat, but she made it clear that was not going to happen. "I will be outside soon and we can take those dead men back to their village."

"Whoa, what is this 'we'? Who said anything about *you* going?" Tall Tree wanted to know.

"We shall see, then." She smiled knowingly before turning to her bag of water for cleaning. "And do hurry, you two. Food first, then question the prisoner. So go!"

The men made not attempt to hide their departure from her tepee. They were only a few feet from the entrance when Soaring Eagle spoke. "Look. Somebody covered the man. Probably just as well, or he might have frozen to death. Probably your Little Crane. She cannot stand to see anything suffer. When I have done the morning games of 'avoid getting dressed' and 'I do not want to eat' and 'brother has my moccasins,' then I will be back and we can question him."

Summer Swan dressed quickly, determined to get to the captive before the men did, but Tall Tree was already talking to him when she exited her tepee. She pulled her buffalo coat tightly around her body and ran her fingers though her tussled hair as she walked. It became apparent that Tall Tree has having not luck getting answers from the man. Soaring Eagle strode toward them, followed by a pair of running boys who fell every few steps.

The prisoner reply to every question with a simple, "I need to pass water."

"Answer our questions and we will cut your ropes," said Tall Tree.

Summer Swan stepped in front of the men and turned to face them. Her voice was low enough that no one could hear her argue with the Chief. "What is the matter with you two? If my water was hurting me to let go, I would not answer either. Let him loose and then ask him your questions."

Soaring Eagle shrugged and pulled away the robe covering the man's body, exposing his complete nudity. It was obvious that his need was great as his large penis stood erect with the morning display. Soaring Eagle cut the sinew tying him to the tree truck. The man sat up and grabbed his penis, aiming it away as he released his flow that seemed to go on forever. He grabbed the robe and pulled it back over himself as he lay down again.

Summer Swan walked to where his clothes lay on the ground where they fell as the warriors cut them off his body. She took them to him and offered them. He reached out one hand and pulled the shredded buckskin under the robe. Soon his body would warm them enough for him to try to put them on. When he did, she could find something to hold the pieces together.

In the meantime, she sat at the far end of the log away from his head. He looked at her and nodded twice. She smiled and returned his nod. The two men who shared her bed and body just a few minutes ago did not miss this exchange.

"Summer Swan, why do you smile and nod at this man? He is nothing. Perhaps you should question him as you did his friend yesterday," suggested Soaring Eagle.

"If you wish, I will." She walked to the prone man and asked, "Who are you? Why did you attack us? What did you want?"

"I am Porcupine Bear, chief of my tribe. We attacked you in search of food. We were not prepared for the winter, at least a winter such as this. Our hunts failed to provide enough game to feed our people. The buffalo have not returned and we cannot find the large animals we need. A few rabbits and such are not sufficient to nourish us all. We feed the children and wet women first, but even they are still hungry."

The men watched in amazement as the prisoner directed his answer to Summer Swan only. There was some bond they sensed between the woman and the man called Porcupine Bear.

Tall Tree started to ask a question, but Soaring Eagle touched his hand and the question never left his lips.

"Continue, Porcupine Bear." Summer Swan offered him a skin of fresh water that he sat up to drink, his eyes never leaving her face.

"Our scouts ventured farther and farther away from our camp, sometimes coming back with a skinny goat or starving antelope, but it was still not enough. One scout never did return and another came back wounded by wolves, which have grown bold with hunger they attacked, just as we have."

Soaring Eagle asked, "Why did you think it necessary to attack us? All you had to do is approach us with friendship and we would have offered help. It might not have been a whole buffalo, but we would have given you food."

Porcupine Bear ignored him and continued to stare at Summer Swan. "Is it true you have food to share? My people are cold and hungry. I will lead you there, if you promise no ill will come to them."

"I cannot make such a promise, as I am just a lowly woman." That caused smiles from the two men and a few outright laughs from other tribe members who had wandered up. "Our chief, Soaring Eagle," she pointed at him, "and the council will have to decide. I must go now and prepare food with the other women." She rose and left the men alone, but she slyly watched them all as she worked.

Soaring Eagle cut the man loose and sat on the log beside him. Someone asked about the buffalo robe covering him, but he ignored the question, instead choosing to tell of his people and village.

When the food was ready, Summer Swan sent Little Crane to tell the men. She waited until all were eating before she moved quietly to one of the storage shelters where she began to select food for transporting. Pemmican, jerky, dried vegetables and fruits, and robes and blankets. She led a pair of packhorses to the shelter and loaded her selections, tying them down tightly. She led them near the village center where the men were finishing their meal. She ate quickly and continued across the open area to her tepee where she dressed in her warmest clothing and packed assorted other items of apparel to take to the other tribe.

Only Tall Tree, Soaring Eagle, and Curved Bear Claw mounted with Porcupine Bear who was leading the horse carrying his dead friends. The other warriors would remain to protect the village. There was no taking a chance on having it invaded and destroyed, as it was the last time. The only warrior who seemed surprised as she mounted her horse was Porcupine Bear. She pulled her horse up beside his as they departed the camp.

Chapter 27

Porcupine Bear was taller than anyone in her village here or the one from which she was abducted as a young woman. When she commented to him about his height, he replied that all is people are tall. "I think it because our ancestors came from the west, far away, where the trees themselves are as tall as the sky. I do not know why they left there, but I hope to travel there someday."

"Trees as tall as the sky?" she asked. "Taller even than the mighty oaks, like the one on the hill to the north of our village? It has been dying for years, but still offers some small shade with its few remaining leaves. It is surrounded now by its many offspring."

"Yes. According to our tales, those trees are higher than any of our hills."

Summer Swan looked back at the pair riding behind her and the other chief. "Did you hear, Soaring Eagle? His people came from a place where the trees are as tall as the sky. It is hard to imagine, I think."

"I have also heard of such trees," said Tall Tree. "Man of Horses told us of a race of people like us, but not like us, who lived among the mountains that run to the sea, far to the west."

No one spoke, but her lovers knew that Summer Swan was thinking of those trees, of the mountains, and a sea that they could not even imagine. She was so full of dreams, they knew, that it would be like her to simply mount her horse and ride off to find them. They looked at one another in complete understanding, each wondering how or if they could stop her if she decided to leave them. She was a free woman bound to no man.

The second afternoon of travel brought them to the village of Porcupine Bear's people. They had camped the night before by a small lake, frozen over with ice so thick a tomahawk could not break it. Never did any of them remember a winter so cold. There had been little snow, which would melt easily for water. This ice was more difficult. The horses smelled water and showed their disapproval by whinnying and stomping their feet. Even the grass was frozen, further distressing the mounts.

Their campfire was small and weak as it took so long for the wood to warm enough to burn. The men did the cooking as Summer Swan wandered away in search of whatever she could find of use.

Porcupine Bear asked, "Why are we cooking? Why isn't the woman at least helping us?"

Soaring Eagle took some time before answering. "She is not like other women. She has some abilities to communicate with the gods, like a shaman. She knows how to heal, like a medicine man. She understands things without being told. She hears things no one else can hear. She dreams things that happen. She is strong of will and body, in a way it is hard to describe. She loves hard and hates even harder."

"She is the one who covered you, we think." Tall Tree said. "We have no idea why she did that, after killing your friend in the manner of a man. Perhaps it was to keep you alive long enough to find your village. She would not be able to let them die of hunger, any more than we would. But she is all woman who takes what she wants from men, and enjoys it more than any other female I have ever known."

"Ah," said Porcupine Bear, "You speak like a man with experience with her. Is she your wife?"

"She is no man's wife, at least not yet," he replied. "She has refused both of us, but gives her love to us, but only together. She is incredible. You shall see."

"Does that mean I can bed her, too?"

"That is her decision, hers alone."

Summer Swan knew they were discussing her, even from the far distance she had traveled from the campsite. She closed her eyes and listened to the wind, blowing from them in her direction. While some words were lost, she picked out enough to understand what they were saying. She smiled. Yes, she was all those things and more.

Over the years I watched Summer Swan. From her first days with the tribe, it became apparent to me that she was special in a number of ways. She kept to herself while she listened to the animals and talked to the Gods. She communicated with the dead as she sat beside their earthly bodies on the platforms. It seemed to me that she did not want the others to know what she could do. At first, I thought it was so that the tribe would not think her a bad spirit, but later I changed my mind. I think she was afraid, at first, of her abilities and needed time to learn to trust herself with such important but uncanny talents.

Summer Swan noted a movement out of the corner of her eye. She stood still like the rocks around her. Turning so slowly even the creature ignored her, she finally made eye contact with the wolf foraging just a few yards from her. He was downwind and missed her odor. She could see he was injured and probably rejected from his pack, left to die on his own.

A wave of sadness swept over her. No one should end his life neglected and unloved like this. She stepped closer to him to use her knife to end his suffering, but he did not run. She saw why. Two of his legs were broken and bones protruded through the skin. He was in pain, no doubt, and too weak even to try to bite her as she approached. From her skirt pocket, she took a small piece of jerky that she placed by his nose and then opened her hand for him to take.

She knew he would die soon if she did nothing to help him. She must reset his legs first. She left him and ran back to the camp. She looked back to see him trying to follow her, limping and swaying and falling. Both injured legs were on the same side, making each limping step an agony. Her eyes filled with tears. She yelled for the men to bring water and food, but they looked at her as if senses were gone. Soaring Eagle reached for his bow and an arrow to shoot the wolf he thought was chasing her.

"No! No! No! Do not shoot him. Bring water and something for him to eat." Her voice was ragged from running. "We must save him."

Tall Tree did what she asked and raced to meet her. Together they turned to meet the starving animal. At their approach, the wolf bared his fangs and growled at Tall Tree. Summer Swan motioned him to stop. She took the water from him and knelt beside the creature, which let her dribble water into its mouth.

"Throw me some jerky or something. He is starved." She tore the dried pemmican into pieces and fed him slowly, a bite at a time. He looked at her with sparkling eyes as if he was crying along with her.

At the campfire, Porcupine Bear watched, shaking his head with lack of understand. "Why is she saving that wolf? He will turn on her any second and kill her without qualms."

Soaring Eagle looked at him before answering. "Why did she save you? You might have turned on her and killed her, too, but you did not. Why?"

The other man looked at the ground. It was a fair question, but one he could not answer.

Soaring Eagle said with a smile, "If I know her, she will want to mend the wolf. We had better start shipping the ice because she will want hot water."

Tall Tree joined them at the lake edge. All three men chipped the ice with their tomahawks until a small stream of water began to flow from under it. They filled their water bags first, and then led the horses to the tiny stream, hoping there was enough for them to drink. Finally, they took bowls to fill the small pot, which Summer Swan had set on a tripod she had made of frozen branches she found on the ground. Her fire was blazing and heat radiated. The wolf lay beside her as she sat on a rock waiting for the water to warm.

She filled a bowl with warm water and added some herbs from her medicine pouch. "Drink this, Sad Wolf, and I will try to help you. You must not hurt me or the men who will help me. Do you understand?" He looked at her and she knew he would not hurt her, now or ever.

She gently petted his dirty coat. She removed burrs and sticks while she waited for him to become sleepy. How much herb to give him was a problem so she guessed, hoping it was not too much, but plenty to cut his pain.

When the water was warm, she washed both legs, cutting away the fur. He began to snore gently, much to the relief of the three men whom she had ordered to help her. She cut through the skin of one leg to expose the place of the break. They were stronger than she was so she had two of them pull each side of the leg while she carefully pushed the shattered section back in place. She washed it carefully again and then spread something from her bag all around it. She pressed dried leaves tightly against it before wrapping it with tanned leather. She tied sinew around the first leg and moved to the other end of the animal to do the same with the second leg.

She ate little that the men had prepared, saving the meat for the wolf. While they waited for him to awaken, she continued cleaning his fur and stroking his head. When he opened his eyes, Porcupine Bear jumped up and backed away. Tall Tree and Soaring Eagle remained sitting, but alert. The wolf looked up and took the shred of meat Summer Swan offered him before sticking out his tongue to lick her face. She hugged his big head to her bosom and smiled through her tears.

Chapter 28

Porcupine Bear was up long before the sun. He was anxious to complete the journey to his village. For the first time, he mentioned that is wife Snake Maiden was with child and her time was near. "He will be tall like me and smart like his mother," he joked.

Soaring Eagle laughed. "Have you thought it might not be a boy?"

The man looked as though the thought was too foreign to him to consider. "Of course, it will be a boy. My dreams tell me so. I have seen him as a child, a man, even as an old man. He looks just like me. No, it is not a girl child."

Tall Tree smiled as he said, "So was my child. Her name is Little Crane."

"Stop talking. We need to ride. It is still a long way." He did not wait, but rode at a slow gallop, leaving them behind. They mounted but followed at a slower pace.

"If it is that far, we will travel at a lesser pace. Not point in tiring the horses," said Soaring Eagle. He watched the limping wolf, walking as best he could beside Summer Swan's horse, waiting for what he knew she would ask.

It was hardly a breath later that she stopped her horse. She dismounted, bent, and tried to pick up the wolf. She got him to waist level, but could not lift him to the top of her skittish horse that wanted no part of the wolf. She put him back on the ground and moved to the front of her mount, rubbing his head and whispering in his ear. He calmed a bit but continued to look in askance at the canine.

Soaring Eagle gave a big sigh as he dismounted. "Get on your horse and I will hand him up to you. But, if he so much as growls at me, he is one dead dog. He is one heavy, even skinny as he is, must weight as much as I do. Good thing I am so strong," He flexed his arms to display muscles covered my layers of clothing.

The wolf made no sound nor gesture as the man lifted him to lie across the horse in front of the woman. He seemed to smile as he covered her face in drooling licks. Summer Swan hugged the wolf, smiled at the men, and said, "Thank you, Soaring Eagle. I am sorry I cannot admire your muscles right now, but I do recall feeling them before. And yours, as well, Tall Tree. Maybe when we get home..." she let her voice trail off. She turned her gaze back to the wolf and reached around to comfort the horse before urging it to a gait.

Porcupine Bear was waiting for them by a rill of water, mostly frozen. "By the gods, we have to wait for you to load that damn wolf? I cannot believe it! I am in a hurry to get home, but you waste time over a useless wolf."

Her face showed no emotion but her voice held anger. "You would not be in such of a hurry if you had not wasted time attacking us instead of asking for help. You would not be in a hurry if you had told us the truth in the first place. If you feel slowed, then we can easily turn around and return to our home with the food we have on the packhorse. The choice is yours."

He did not reply, but mounted his horse and rode off ahead of them. "He reminds me of a sulking child, rather than a chief," she said.

It was dusk when they smelled the smoke of campfires. Porcupine Bear kicked his horse into a full run, leaving them behind. They stopped in a grove of bare trees by a frozen lake, larger than the one they used the day before. Tall Tree reached gently lifted the wolf from the horse and Summer Swan slid to the ground. She urged the canine to follow her and watched his pain as limped behind her. She secreted him in some thick bushes and gave him water and more pemmican. "Now, stay here, my friend, until I come for you. Make no noise and let no person see you. Do you understand?" She hoped he did because he could not run away and he would die if spotted. She petted him one last time before joining her lovers for the final portion of their journey.

The village was a dismal place. The tepees had holes and bent supports and several looked abandoned. The ground was rocky and uneven, not cleared of stones and leveled as their own was. The fire pit was small. There were no piles of wood or buffalo chips anywhere. No food hung over the dying coals. The only smoke came from just four tepees and in the distance; they could see the burial platforms tilted and falling down. The trio exchanged glances, before Soaring Eagle called out a greeting.

In reply came a pathetic scream of a woman in one of the tepees where there was a fire. Summer Swan ran to it, pushing through the flap without knocking. On the ground near the fire lay a young woman, legs apart, straining to give birth. Porcupine Bear crouched beside her. When he saw Summer Swan he yelled, "Do something. If you are a shaman or medicine man or whatever you are, help her. She is dying and my son has not come out yet."

She knelt beside the woman, pushing Porcupine Bear aside. "Hello, I am Summer Swan and I will try to help you." She took the woman's hand and felt only a dim pulsating on her wrist. "She is more dead than alive."

Soaring Eagle and Tall Tree were standing behind her. Tall Tree handed her you medicine pouch. Porcupine Bear screamed at her again. "Get my son out of her. If you have to cut her open, do it. She will die anyway."

Summer Swan moved so quickly no one saw her hand as it struck the screaming man across the face, but all heard it. The blow was strong enough to knock him backward. He jumped back up, armed with his knife as he moved to Summer Swan. Two other knives blocked him and forced him backward to the door and out.

Chapter 29

"Do you have warm water," Summer Swan demanded. "And some clean cloths?" No one replied. She looked around the room. Against one side was a woman so wrinkled she could have been a hundred winters or more. Two young women huddled together under sleeping blankets.

"Is there anyone who can help me? Can you get water and rags?" Finally, one of the young women arose. She was so thin she seemed little more than bones with skin over them. She handed some dirty cloths to Summer Swan and hurried back under the blankets. Summer Swan called to the men outside. "I need water and some clean scraps of skins." Tall Tree was by her side in a minute with what she asked.

"Is she dead? She looks like it. Why is she here instead of out by herself to give birth?" he wanted to know.

"I do not know, but I suspect she was too ill to leave. Surely, she would have frozen anyway. No one here seems to care if she lives or dies."

The woman screamed again, pushing to purge her body of the child, but nothing moved between her legs. Her head dropped to the side as she drew her last breath. Summer Swan reached inside the spread legs to feel for the child. Its back faced the birth canal, not its head, or even its butt. Knowing the woman was past feeling, she pushed both her hands and arms into the abdomen, pushed the bones apart, and pulled as hard as she could. The child shot out like a cannon ball into Summer Swan's lap.

The woman bit the cord. She held the child by the ankles and slapped its tiny, nearly blue bottom. A faint whimper came from the baby. Summer Swan pushed her fingers deep within the child's mouth, into its throat, and pulled mucus from it. She pressed one hand on the back and pressed as she breathed tiny breaths into the mouth. Suddenly the child convulsed a blockage from its lungs and began crying in earnest.

Porcupine Bear rushed inside. "Let me see my son." He reached for the child, but stepped back when Summer Swan held it up for him to see. He had a daughter. "This cannot be. I dreamed of my son. A daughter is useless."

He was shaking hard and pushed the child away with such force that Summer Swan almost dropped it. "You do not deserve a son, or a daughter either. You are a cruel man. What you dreamed was of yourself, your time as a child, an adult, and an old man you might have become, but you will not live that long. I foresee you succumbing to a pack of wolves, which is no better than you deserve. Leave this child and go."

He left the tepee, ran to his horse, and rode away. "He will not return," Summer Swan said to her tribesmen. "He has displeased the gods and he will die soon. And so will the child if we cannot feed her."

Chapter 30

A few people crept out of their tents at the smell of food cooking over the community fire pit. Tall Tree found buffalo chips a far distance from the village and Soaring Eagle started a fire with things he found abandoned at the perimeter of the place. Summer Swan came out of the tepee carrying the child in her arms.

"This child has no mother. The woman is dead. Is there anyone here who can take her and feed her?" No one answered. "Is no woman a wet woman?"

An ancient man, bent with age, spoke in a crackling voice. "Speckled Fawn has a child."

"Who is Speckled Fawn? Where is she?"

A small woman carrying a child in her arms stepped from her tent. "I am. But I have no milk to spare. My son needs more than I can give him, so I have none for another child."

Looking at the skinny young woman, Summer Swan was sure there would be none for the newborn. "Perhaps we can change that. If you have more to eat, you will produce more milk."

"How am I to do that? We have nothing to eat but what roots we can find on the plain. We have no meat and there is no game here. The cold has killed everything, including many of our tribe. And you have killed our men." She pointed to the horse with the bodies tied to it. "One of them was my husband." Her face filled with hate as she looked at Tall Tree and Soaring Eagle.

Soaring Eagle's voice was soft as he answered her. "They would still be alive if they had not attacked our village. We do not have many supplies, but we would have shared if they had asked. We did not want to fight, but your warriors left us no choice. Only your chief chose to tell us of your needs rather than die a slow death."

Speckled Fawn looked confused. "Our chief is not dead. He is there." She pointed at the wizardly old man who had spoken earlier.

"Who was the man that just rode away? He said he was your chief, Porcupine Bear."

The Old Man moved to a rock by the fire. His knees crackled as he sat. "I am Chief Big Bull. The man Porcupine Bear was my stepson. He will never be chief. He is cruel and no one likes him, even the poor woman he gave a child. He was not her husband. He took her because she was beautiful and afraid of him and now she is dead and he does not care." A look of sadness crossed his face. "She was my granddaughter."

Summer Swan looked around her as the men joined Big Bull and talked. There were only young men, probably left behind to defend the village. Several women moved forward and took the food offered. They fed their emaciated children first, then themselves. They ate little which Summer Swan was sure was the norm for them. Always warriors and children ate first, but here it was apparent no one ate their fill.

When everyone had eaten, Soaring Eagle spoke. "There is some meat left. We do not want the night scavengers to get it, so please finish it. We have more for morning and the next days, too." He did not have to say it twice. Within minutes, all was gone and many stomach felt fullness for the first time in months.

He continued. "Your chief Big Bull has agreed that it is best for you to come back with us and join our tribe. You will be treated no differently than our own people. You are not slaves. You are free to come or go as you wish. We have young men in need of wives. You have you women wanting husbands. Your shaman is gone. We have Summer Swan who is like no other woman. Those of you who wish to come with us, we welcome you. If you choose to stay behind, we wish you luck and prosperity. We will leave in two mornings as soon as you are ready."

He looked at Summer Swan who slowly rose from a rock where she sat cuddling the tiny baby. "What I say may sound harsh and maybe even cruel, but it must be said. Most of your tepees are in such poor condition that they are unlivable. You can cut them up to save the good portions for other uses. Take down the strong lodge pole, along with things of use. Cracked cooking pots and the like are not worth the time. We will help you replace them at our village.

"It will take at least two days to get to our village. If there are not enough horses, you will have to ride several to a horse, children can easily do that. The old and weak must ride, but those strong enough can walk. On the way, our men and your young men can hunt and the women will help me find herbs and roots. Tomorrow we will help you build your burial platforms for the dead, and repair those falling. We will celebrate tomorrow and thank the gods for directing us to you and for your new life with us."

There were some hoots and laughter when she stopped talking. Speckled Fawn, carrying a tightly covered baby, walked shyly toward Summer Swan. She held her arms out, offering her child, and took the tiny girl from Summer Swan. She sat on the rock at their feet, opened her shirt, and put the child to her breast. A bond between the two women formed at that moment. It was a bond that would last a lifetime.

Chapter 31

Everyone who was able was out before the sun was up. Some wrapped the dead woman for burial while the majority went to the burial ground to repair the platforms and make room for the new body. Speckled Fawn took both children to her tepee the night before and sat nursing them as Summer Swan entered. "I will stay with the babes while you go out for something to eat," she said. "Then I have an errand to do. I have a four footed friend outside the village. He was hurt and hungry and waits for me to bring him food and water and check his wounds."

"Why did you not bring him with you? It would be easier for you if you had," asked Speckled Fawn.

Summer Swan laughed. "I doubt he would have been welcomed. He is a mangy, old wolf."

"A wolf! By the gods, he will attack you. If he is hungry, he will eat you. Do your men know about this? Send them to destroy the animal." Speckled Fawn was obviously upset and afraid.

"He will not hurt me. Nor has he harmed the men. It would frighten your people too much to have him here, but when we leave tomorrow morning, he will go with us. I will try to keep him away as far as possible. Now, give me the children and get some food. We have to fatten you up if you are going to feed two starving mouths."

Later Summer Swan approached the bushes where she had hidden. There was no sign of her Sad Wolf. She called softly to him. Finally, from a distance away she heard his soft reply. She turned to watch him limp toward her, amazed that he was doing so well. He gulped down the meat she gave him and drank his fill of water. He licked her face and lay down beside her. She carefully removed the wrapping on his legs and tossed away the inside packing to expose the lacerated areas. "My Man, you are already starting to heal. We will put some new herbs on you and pack it back tight. You must stay hidden, not go out roaming around, or for sure you will be killed. Tomorrow we will return to my village. Do you understand?" She laughed as he licked her face again, as if to say he did. She petted him and cleaned his fur again before returning to help with plans for the move in the morning.

The day went fast with moving preparations. Excitement was infectious and everyone was in high spirits. All tummies were full for the second day in a row, which contributed to sleepy eyes and an early evening. The night before, Summer Swan slept with the babes and Speckled Fawn and as she headed toward the tepee, Soaring Eagle reached for her hand and pulled her to him. Tall Tree moved up behind her to slide his hand between them to cup her tits.

She smiled. "Are you two going to rape me? Is that what you have in mind, because I do not recall inviting either one of you into my blankets this night."

Tall Tree nuzzled the back of her neck, under her thick hair, moving his tongue to relish her salty dried tastes. The other man pressed his lips to her, moving them so slowly it took her breath away. She opened her mouth to accept his tongue as the fingers pressing her nipples increased their pressure. She sighed deeply and moved away from them.

Neither of the men moved. She nodded and took a hand from each to press to her cheeks, licking them in turn. "Where?" was the only thing she said? They were prepared, as she found, when they led her to the tepee of the dead woman. Everything was gone but some fresh sleeping blankets and a small fire nearby.

The men removed their heavy buffalo coats. The fire had warmed the tepee, even though there were tears in places that allowed cold air to enter. They pushed their coats into those holes then took hers for the same purpose. They removed their clothes and plugged more places as she admired their taut, muscular bodies in the flickering firelight.

They turned to her, but she pushed them away. Slowly, seductively, she dropped her skirt to show the winter undergarment made of fuzzy buffalo that hid her womanhood from them. The shirt went over her head and her nipples hardened in the coolness of the tepee. She walked to them and put her hand behind each head, pushing it down so the mouths covered the ends of her tits. She let her head fall backward as she arched her chest to meet their tongues and teeth.

"Harder," she whispered. "Suck them harder. Bite them gently at the same time. Oh, by the gods, that is good." They moved against her, pressing their throbbing cocks against her stomach. She caught one in each hand and skimmed the smooth skins up and down, feeling the excitement grow in them. She sank to her knees to kiss the tips of first one rock-hard penis, then the other. They were a bit different in length and size, but tasted somewhat the same. Neither was better in any way, either inside her mouth or inside her wet, oh so dripping pussy.

But now was to tease their rock-hard penises. She sucked one until she felt its throb told it the man was close to erupting, then moved her mouth to pleasure the other. At the same time, she jacked up and down on the other one, taking time to squeeze the balls as well. When she was sure that a climax was near, she switched her actions from one man to the other again. The groans from both became so frequent that she skimmed them both in her hands while her lips moved from one tip to the other. As if on cue, the two men came at the same time. She directed their semen downward to her breasts, which sparkled with cum in the firelight.

The men dropped to the sleeping blanket and sat watching her as she rubbed their wet seed all over her tits. She moved her hands down to untie the garment covering her womanhood. She stood before them, offering herself without bounds. Tall Tree put his arms around her hips and pulled her to him. He dipped his head so he could reach her mound with his tongue.

Soaring Eagle moved behind her and rubbed her puckered tits, squeezing and pinching them the way he knew she liked. She arched her back to push hard against Tall Tree's mouth, crying out as he found his target. Her little clit was growing, both longer and wetter. He sucked and licked it, using his teeth gently to pull it into his mouth as far as he could. Her hips began to rock. Soaring Eagle bent over her prone body to worship her tits. Her low moans excited them both and they were ready again. But first, it was time to give their love to Summer Swan. They kept pleasuring her until she exploded, pouring her wetness into the mouth that brought her such wonderful release.

She collapsed forward over Tall Tree's head. Soaring Eagle gently picked her up and laid her on the blankets. He spread her legs and inserted his hard-again cock into her, just a fraction at a time. It teased him as much as it did her and gave her time to regain her desires. She turned her face to Tall Tree's cock, which was beside her head, bobbing up and down as he caressed it. She took it from him and began to play with it, increasing its size and excitement. Her hips moved to meet Soaring Eagle's slow entrance into her mons and deeper into her vagina.

Her lips and mouth gave pleasure to Tall Tree as her pussy captivated Soaring Eagle. Movement became rapid. Breathing became rapid. Blood ran rapid through their veins. In the distance, a wolf howled as they all three reached their climaxes.

Chapter 32

She awoke to the pressure of her thighs separating under tender hands. She was on her back and pretended to sleep. Slowly, so wonderfully slow, the penis moved into her. The tip was wet and soon found more wetness as it slid deeper into her. She moaned, as if in her sleep, and spread her legs wider. As the man above her increased his motions, it became harder for her to lay still. She wanted him to think she did not know he was fucking her. Did it seem like rape to him, was that what he wanted? Well, she would let him think so and did not move. But her pussy gave her away by contracting and releasing his cock to meet his rhythm.

"Stop pretending and start enjoying it. I know you are awake." Tall Tree did not have to tell her twice. She wrapped her legs around his hips and rode with him until he released his seed deeply into her.

Her eyes were still closed when he pulled out of her. In an instant, Soaring Eagle took his place. He slid his fingers inside of her touching her clit even as he continued to move in and out. He rubbed the semen left by his friend all around her pussy, mostly on her throbbing little pearl. This time, she reached her climax almost immediately. Her lover followed before her body stopped quivering.

He rolled off and lay beside her. Cum matted nether hair that came from her as well as the two men. Tall Tree knelt between her legs and gently washed away the glistening droplets from their three-way sex. Summer Swan drew a quick breath as his thumb found her clit again. It pressed a bit harder and moved in a wider circle, teasing her until again she arched to meet his hand. Her second climax was incredible and she cried out her pleasure. When her hips returned to the blanket, she was exhausted and out of breath. Each man kissed her lips, already swollen from last night, and dressed as he looked down at her.

"Stay and rest for a few minutes. We will start the fire and food. It is the least we can do after 'raping' you in your sleep," said Tall Tree.

"Well," she answered, "if that was rape, then I will let you know when I want to be 'raped' again." After they took their heavy robes from the holes in the tepee, the place filled with cold air immediately. "So much for resting." She hurried into her clothes and pulled her robe from the tepee walls. As she reached for the door flap, she heard a low growl from behind the tepee. She moved to the other side and looked down through one of the holes. There sat Sad Wolf, wagging his tail as he looked up at her.

"What are you doing here?" The worn old buffalo skin ripped apart easily in her hands. It was easy for her to rip it down until he could step inside. He licked her face and nuzzled her. When his greeting was complete, he used his teeth to pull at the covers on his back leg. "Is it hurting, boy?" she asked. Carefully she untied the sinew and unwrapped the packing. To her amazement, the wound appeared partially healed and the swelling was gone. She did the same to the front leg and felt relief that it too appeared much better. She hugged the wolf around the neck until he backed away and retreated outside the tepee. He sat there as if waiting for her to follow, which she did.

Before she had a chance to announce his presence, the children and women screamed and ran to their tepees. Several young warriors put arrows to their bow as she yelled for them to stop. They did not heed her shout, so she dropped to the ground beside the canine and wrapped her arms around him. To shoot the wolf would risk shooting Summer Swan and no one wanted to do that.

Chief Big Bull walked toward her and the wolf. He gait was slow. His eyes met those of the wolf, each unwavering. When he reached them, he offered his hand to the creature, which smelled him before licking his hand. The villagers had never seen anything like it before and began to all talk at once.

Summer Swan stood and Tall Tree and Soaring Eagle moved quickly to each side of her.

"He will not hurt you," said the old chief. "See how he is with the newcomers. I do not understand it myself, but the wolf belongs to the woman and the men with her. No one is to harm him. He is a sign from the gods that what we do today is what is meant to be. So, quickly, let us prepare for our journey and the place of our new home."

They dismantled the entire camp and loaded the usable things in bundles tied to their horses. Small children rode with the pregnant women. Every horse carried not only riders but as many bundles as it could carry. Ordinarily, travois would follow the horses, but the tribe was so poor that they were of no use, with a few exceptions. One exception was for the lodge poles and outsides of the good tepees and the other was for two ill persons who lay together, bound to their travois.

Summer Swan knew the sick pair would not survive the journey, probably not even the night. One was a woman so old no one could even guess her years and the other a child of about four who had multiple birth defects and a strange discoloration to his body. Nothing she gave him did anything to help, but she tried. He had been unconscious for several days, they said, but she tried to save him and shared the pain that his mother felt. The death of a child always hurt her in ways she could not explain, even to herself. The father of the child was on the burial platform they left behind. They would place the dead on burial platforms when they reached camp.

Healthy women and most warriors walked, along with children old enough to take the miles they crossed each day. Tall Tree and Soaring Eagle rode their horses far from the travelers and were lucky enough to kill a few rabbits and snakes that poked their heads out of dens in order to bask in the sun, which gave little warmth to anyone.

Late on second afternoon just at sunset, Summer Swan wandered far from the people. She searched for herbs and roots in the frozen miles of the plains. At an iced-over creek, she used her knife to break into the water below. She knelt on her knees to drink from her hand, which she used to scoop up the icy water. She heard a small noise behind her but before she could turn, a hand covered her mouth and a knife pressed tightly against her neck.

"So, the perfect woman is too stupid to hear my movements. That is as it should be, because you are not a shaman or medicine woman. You are just another bag with tits and a slot for my cock. I want to hear you cry for me to kill you, because the pain I will give you will be more than you can take. Now stand up, slowly."

Without looking, she knew it was Porcupine Bear. "Why are you doing this? All you have to do is join the rest of us and start a new life in our village."

"Ha, do you think anyone will ever forget the things I have done? The way I stole the old man's granddaughter and used her, will they forget that? No. And the others who disappeared, will they stop thinking I was the one who took them? No. All things wrong, they blame on me."

"Did you take the ones who disappeared? Did you do the things they think you did?"

He laughed. "Yes, I did. I like the girls before they reached bleeding age. They were so soft and tender. I loved the way their tightness brought me bliss. You have not idea what that is like. You are like an old sow that will die like one when I am finished with you. Now, take off your clothes."

"I will not. If you want them off me, then you remove them. I will not help you."

Instead of replying, he grabbed her hand and slashed her palm. "Next time, I will cut it off."

Still Summer Swan did not move. She let her hand fall and felt the blood dripping down her fingers onto the frozen ground. He moved toward her, reaching again for her hand. Suddenly, from behind him came a growl, deep in the throat of a large, leaping wolf that knocked him to the ground in a second. From all around, Summer Swan heard more growls and saw several shapes in the dark shadows of the early night. She stepped back, away from the man on the ground as the pack began to tear him apart. She stood calmly as he screamed, but she felt no remorse. The gods saw he got his punishment.

One wolf moved away from the others and bumped his head to her hips. She knelt beside him and hugged him close. "You are whole again and back with your own. I am happy for you. Can you thank them for me for saving my life?"

The creature licked her hand, washing away the blood. She stood, tears in her eyes, as she patted his head. "Goodbye, my friend." Sad Wolf understood and walked behind her until she reached the encampment before turning to race back to his own kind.

Chapter 33

I watched the ragtag band approach the village. Scouts saw them the day before and reported that Soaring Eagle, Tall Tree, and Summer Swan were returning. I did not hear until later the story of the wolves and the man who claimed to be a chief. A new woman used herbs from Summer Swan's medicine bag to apply to the deep knife cut in her had. The newcomers were proud that one of them had done a good thing for all, thus making their entrance into the tribe less of a poverty issue and more of an equal merger.

That was nonsense I knew, but Summer Swan made quite a big thing of it. She could have done it herself, but as usual, she was kind. Well, most of the time, she was kind. Remember the enemy she castrated, remember the ones she stabbed in cold blood to protect the children and Tall Tree. In the years that followed, she never ceased to amaze me, but you will see for yourself as my tale continues.

Tepees went up in record time, as the temperature seemed to drop even more. In the home of Man of Horses, old Chief Big Bull, Speckled Fawn and the two babies made it their place, with the blessing of Soaring Eagle. Soaring Eagle welcomed the elder as a chief, equal in all ways. The old man nodded slowly and took a seat beside the others around the campfire.

* * * *

Later, when most people retired for the night, Soaring Eagle asked Tall Tree to take a walk with him. "We need to discuss something that has been on my mind for several days. No, for several weeks."

Little Crane came to snuggle in Tall Tree's lap until she became drossy and kissed him goodnight before returning to the tepee of Sweet Flower and the 'terrible twins,' as she called them now. They were walking and knew no bounds, other than the sharp words of Summer Swan who was the only one who had any control over them. They were adorable and amusing to everyone, but totally lacked discipline. Soaring Eagle knew he must be the one to teach them, but their bright eyes and sweet smiles instantly turned his heart to mush. Each night he vowed to himself that the next morning he would start on the unwanted task, but each morning a pair of rough and tumble little scamps jumped onto his sleeping robes to wrestle. It was hard to make them behave when he was laughing.

He told this to Tall Tree who laughed. "Do I not turn into a soft kitten whenever Little Crane turns those big eyes at me and smiles that smile that melts me every time? If this is what your want to discuss, it can surely wait until morning. I am tired and you should be. Summer Swan…"

Soaring Eagle interrupted him. "Yes, let's walk. She is what I want to talk to you about."

They wrapped their winter robes tightly around to shut out the incredibly cold air of the night. "Do you remember asking me moons ago about my feelings for Summer Swan?" Soaring Eagle began. "I told you she was her own person and not my possession and you began to spend some nights with her. It was none of my business, but I knew you were beginning to love her and I felt a strange resentment of that."

Tall Tree nodded. "Yes, I have fallen in love with her, but while we enjoy each other at night, she does not love me. Are you asking me to leave her alone?"

"No, my friend. I am not asking that. I am asking if you have noticed any changes in her. Last night she felt different to me. Fuller, perhaps. Her belly seems larger. Is she with child?"

"Soaring Eagle, it is not for me to say, but you are my friend. Yes she is. Beyond that, you must talk to her yourself." He laughed. "At least after the hours we spent with her last night, we do not need to worry about that. By the gods, just thinking of it makes my cock grow. Do you think she would, no probably not."

The next morning when the twins landed on his stomach, knocking the wind out of him, he forced his face into a stern demeanor. "Now, starting today, young men, you are going to change your ways. First, have you eaten? Good. Go to the water bucket by the door and wash your hands and face. Clean. No, I said clean. Land Hunter, if that is clean, I would hate to see you dirty. Iron Eyes, you are no better. If you are not clean, we cannot go visit a special friend."

That comment got their attention and they returned to vigorously rub their mouths, forgetting there is more to a face that the mouth. It was hard, but Soaring Eagle kept a straight face. He joined them and washed his face just as hard. They watched and mimicked him, actually getting most of the dirt and dried food off.

"Now, straighten your clothes and put your buffalo coats back on." In their gibberish, he detected a phrase of two that made some sense, including one that demanded to know where they were going. "Would you like to guess?" Both little heads nodded and they began to shout out names, a few he could understand. "Alright. Name one person you would most like to see."

It was clear that their mumble-jumble formed something like "Summer Swan." He nodded, pulled on his heavy cloak, picked them both up, and off they went. He whispered to them that they must be quiet and sneak into her tepee without a word, but only after he looked inside first to see that she was there. She was asleep, curled up alone like a beautiful gift from the gods. He motioned the twins to go in and waited until he heard the shouts and giggles and her sleepy voice telling them she loved them.

His plan ended at this point. He stooped his head and went through the flap to join the threesome on her sleeping robes. She was wearing a deerskin shirt that barely covered her, but did afford some warmth in the chilly tepee. He could see patches of bare skin as the boys bounced on top and under the robes. He wanted to reach under the furry covers and let his hands search for her special spots. He wanted to slip in beside her and hold her in his arms.

Why not, he thought. Quickly, he dropped his coat and kicked off his moccasins. He slid under her robe and pulled her into his arms. The boys laughed and rolled around them as he bent his head to press his lips gently on hers. He felt her tense and wondered if she was going to reject him. Instead, she put the tip of her tongue between his lips and slowly moved it in a slow sensual movement that made him instantly hard. She pulled away and grabbed first one's little face between her hands to kiss grinning lips, and then the other.

Soaring Eagle felt her bare legs as he slid his hand down to cup her warm ass. He let his fingers moved upward into the hair between her legs. She moaned deep in her throat before tightening her thighs to hold his hand still. She looked into his eyes, but said not a word. He could not read her expression but knew what his own showed her. He wanted her and he wanted her now.

"Boys, now that Summer Swan is awake, go wake up Little Crane. That should be fun." His voice was deep and his breathing even deeper. In a second, the rambunctious pair ran out and the flap dropped behind them.

Still she did not speak, but her thighs relaxed. He bent his head to kiss her again when she lifted her mouth to meet his. Her arms curled around his neck. Her hands slipped under the back of his shirt. He sat up to pull it off. She reached down to untie his trousers and grasp his throbbing penis in her fingers, moving them slowly up and down the length of him. He pushed up her doeskin dress to expose her tits, taking one then the other in his teeth, nibbling gently. The tips hardened and tightened into peaks that he loved to suck and tease with his tongue. He could feel the roundness of them that had not been there since she suckled the twins.

He tasted her tits and wanted to taste every inch of her. Without removing the rest of their clothes, he drew back the buffalo robe to expose her. Kneeling between her hips, he started at her swollen breast and moved his mouth down her body, using his lips, tongue, and teeth to worship every inch of her. Her odors were pungent and excited him even more. He spread her legs and burrowed his face into her wetness. His tongue found the swollen center of her desires. He continued to lick her until she raised her hips and cried out her ecstasy.

Only then did he allow himself to thrust in gigantic cock into her softness. He moved slowly at first, giving her time to recover from such a climax. She began to match his rhythm, wrapping her legs around his waist. His desire took over and he jabbed into her with increasing speed. He felt his semen spurt into her and silently begged it to never end. End it did, however, leaving him spent, and holding her down with his body. She stirred under him, gently rocking him away.

"Why is it you are not heavy one minute, then weigh more than a buffalo the next?" she asked.

He rolled over onto his back and said, "Do not talk now. Just kiss me and snuggle close to me. You are a she devil who leaves a man with no strength nor desire to move."

They lay together and drifted off to sleep until the sound of little voices came toward them. He jumped up and pulled on his shirt. He was still tying his trousers when the babbling pair rushed inside, each holding one of Little Crane's hands as they dragged her with them. They burst through the flap and dove onto Summer Swan's sleeping robes.

Little Crane looked at their faces, first one and then the other. "Why are your faces so red?" She crinkled her brow as she spoke, as if thinking deeply.

"We were talking and laughing about the twins," replied Summer Swan.

"What did they do that was so funny you laughed until your faces turned red?"

"Ah…I was telling Summer Swan about the chase I had last night getting them to bed," said Soaring Eagle.

"Well, I have put them to bed many times, and I no longer think what they do is so funny," Little Crane frowned as she spoke. "Well, sometimes it is. What did they do this time?"

Soaring Eagle looked at Summer Swan for help and she responded with only a smile. "Well," he said, "when I packed Land Hunter into his night things, Iron Eyes took his own clothes off and began running around naked. I grabbed him and while I was pushing him in his night things, Land Hunter took his off. Iron Eyes wiggled away and took off what I had just put on him. They ran in circles like wild buffalo, so I sat down to wait for them to fall in exhausting. They changed the running into a game where one knelt down and the other jumped over him, then they changed positions and did it all over again. They looked like two little toads, hopping. They laughed so much I finally gave up my stern face and joined them."

Little Crane frowned at him. "I have seen them do that and the first time it was funny. Now it is not fun or funny. And they looked cute like little green frogs not ugly old toads."

"Well, we thought it was," smiled Summer Swan, but not sure that the girl believed the story. "Now, all of you, out! I need to get my clothes on."

She dressed and went outside where Soaring Eagle waited for her on her log. "Summer Swan, let us take a walk for a few minutes. I have something to talk to you about."

"Cannot it wait? I am hungry. You should be, too, after all that exercise you just had."

Soaring Eagle wavered, not sure what to do. He wanted that smile and look of physical satisfaction to remain on her face, but he feared if he refused to eat now, she might not be is such a mood later. But, he wanted to talk to her now, so he took a chance. "Can you wait just a few minutes? This is important."

As he suspected, her face clouded, but she nodded. He took her arm and led her behind her tepee into the grass that was just beginning to sprout, heralding the growing season. "What is more important than eating? Well, Summer Swan, what is more important is this question. Are you with child?"

"You could have waited until my stomach was full of food instead of just baby," she answered. "You know I am easier to get along with when I am not hungry. And the answer is, yes, I am, with child."

He picked her up and spun in a circle, laughing as he did so. Finally, he stopped and set her dizzily on the ground. "Will marry me, Summer Swan?"

Her face was devoid of emotion as she looked up at him. "So, now that I am with child, you want to take me as your wife. Maybe it is Tall Tree's child, did you think of that? Well, forget it, I do not want to marry you. Oh, yes, I did at one time, but you made it clear you would never marry again. I do not need a husband because I caught a baby. Lots of women raise their children without a mate, and I plan to be one of them." She turned and shrugged off the hand he tried to use to grab her hand.

Chapter 34

Her emotions were a mixture of anger and self-pity. She knew her refusal to marry Soaring Eagle was out of spite because it is what she wanted from the first night they shared their bodies with one another. However, in her heart she knew it was only because of the child, not because he loved her. Perhaps she should marry Tall Tree instead. He truly loved her. The problem was that she did not love him the way she loved Soaring Eagle.

Tall Tree was a good man, a great lover, and he would be the better choice. Good choices were not always the ones a person wanted to make. She needed to talk to someone to help her. She could not discuss it with Speckled Fawn because she was sure the young woman loved Tall Tree.

Big Bull was sitting outside his tepee when she returned to the village. "Can I talk to you? I have a problem and want your advice." The old man nodded and patted his log for her to sit beside him. He said nothing and simply waited. "I am with child, Big Bull. Soaring Eagle is the father. He offered to marry me, but he does not love me. Tall Tree loves me and would take my child as his own. I do not know what to do. Maybe I should marry no one. Please tell me what to do."

"Child, I cannot tell you what to do. It is for your heart to decide. I know you enjoy them both, and that is good. Seldom does a woman find two men who are willing to bed her, especially together. That alone should tell you that Soaring Eagle cares for you enough to share you. On the other hand, it could be he enjoys your body and excitement of watching you and his friend. The same is true with Tall Tree.

"There is another solution you might consider, Summer Swan. It is not unheard of in our history, although it has happened seldom. You might marry them both. How you share yourself with them you would have to decide, always with the two of them or separately. It is not a small problem, and you want each man happy, too. You must think long before you make your decision.

"I am sorry, child that I can offer you no answers. All I do know is that you are unhappy now and life is too short for unhappiness." He squeezed her hand and arose to enter his tepee. As he closed the flap, he said, "Perhaps you should talk to the gods."

Summer Swan sat on his log for a long time. Finally, she stood and walked out into the plain toward the burial platforms. Once there, she set the ladder to the side where Man of Horses lay. She climbed the rickety wooden structure and sat cross-legged beside the body. It was not necessary for her to speak aloud to either him or the gods. She looked skyward, but with one hand on his body. This unspoken conversation was for all who wanted to hear. After a while, she closed her eyes and began chanting in a low, sweet voice. The chant was wordless, more a series of sad sounds that came from somewhere deep inside her.

It was midday when she finished and started down the ladder. It happened so quickly that she did not realize it until she felt air under her feet where the rung had been. Below her were two rocks, one large one where her back would hit and a smaller one under her head. The ladder broke and she plummeted down into a pit of darkness.

* * * *

Little Crane hunted everywhere but could not find Summer Swan. It was sunset before she told her father of her futile search. He roused several others who joined him in shouting her name. The shouts aroused Big Bull from his slumber. He stepped outside, cursing himself for sleeping so much, a plight of the old. His eyesight, however, was still strong and as the sun rode low in the western sky, he thought he saw a shape on the ground beside the burial platforms. He knew then that it was Summer Swan who had gone to Man of Horses and to talk to the gods.

He yelled and pointed in that direction. Tall Tree jumped upon his horse and was the first to arrive. He saw the blood between her legs even before he jumped down. As he bent over her motionless body, he saw her chest moving as she took tiny shallow breaths. He stooped to pick her up but stopped when he saw the blood under her head. He turned and yelled at the man nearing him to return for the travois.

Soaring Eagle dropped off his horse even as it still ran. The two men looked at each other, sharing their pain. Gently he turned her to her side to reveal the two wounds. The smaller on her head was only trickling a small stream of blood, but the one in her back was deep and bleeding profusely when they moved her. Apparently, the stone had sealed her wound until her prone body moved. Both men pulled off their loincloths, the only thing they wore during the day in the hot months and pressed the deerskin into the hole to slow the bleeding.

Several others offered their loincloths and whatever else they wore. The women set about finding moss and leaves and herbs. No one knew what they might need but Little Crane, between her tears, pointed out things she picked when hunting for them with Summer Swan. Speckled Fawn tried to remember the things she had seen Summer Swan use on some of the sick or hurt in the months between the cold and the warm seasons.

Tall Tree and Soaring Eagle carefully lifted her onto the travois, positioning her so her back and head wounds were visible. If ever a travois had moved so carefully, it was now. Sweet Flower knew the pain that the ground could cause, so she led the horse herself, watching for rocks, clumps, and anything that might jar the silent woman.

Little Crane walked beside the travois, carefully holding on to Summer Swan's hands. When they reached the woman's tepee, she ran ahead to ready the sleeping robes by placing worn pieces of skins to collect the blood running slowly from the injured woman. She held back the flap as her uncle and father gently carried Summer Swan inside and laid her on the bed. Speckled Fawn followed behind them and dropped the flap down. The tribe's people waited for a while, but soon wandered away to cook and eat as the night closed in around them.

Only Speckled Fawn who was working on Summer Swan and the two men and Little Crane remained. The men sat on the ground cross-legged, never speaking as they watched. Little Crane cried softly until sleep claimed her as she snuggled in her father's arms.

The head wound was easy for Speckled Fawn to clean, medicated, and packed once she had cut away the hair surrounding it. The wound in Summer Swan's back was deep and full of grass, dirt, and other assorted bits of foreign material. As carefully as humanly possible, she used her fingers at first to clean as much as she could. She used her fingernails next, followed by the point of her knife. The darkness of the tepee made it hard for her to see, until Soaring Eagle brought torchlight to her side and held it as she continued to clear the wound.

"Soaring Eagle, can you use your knife like I did to dig out those things? My fingers are stiff and I am shaking. I will hold the torch for you. I think Summer Swan is feeling nothing right now, so if you have to go deep, it should not hurt her."

She took the torch and moved aside for the man to take her place. A great deal of time passed before he asked Tall Tree to take a turn. The rotated places one more time before Speckled Fawn pronounced it as clean as they could get it. The men retreated to the far side of the tepee while she rinsed the wound several times with clear water. Next, she spread several powders from Summer Swan's medicine bag to all surfaces inside.

Little Crane awoke and sat beside the motionless woman while Speckled Fawn stared blankly, completely empty of what to do next. "Can I help?" the little voice asked. "I have watched Summer Swan many times with wounds, like my father had from the knife, and when the children fall or something and hurt themselves."

The adults exchanged glances and nodded. Little Crane drew a deep breath. "Do you see this skinny root? Summer Swan would soak it in water and cut it in little pieces almost as small as sand. She told me it helped the muscles to stop bleeding and would go away once the skin grew back."

It took several minutes for the root to soak up the water and diminish into pieces under the knives of the three adults. Each time one of them thought they were small enough, Little Crane would shake her head. Finally, she deemed them acceptable. She picked them up in her little hand and carefully pressed each into the tissue and muscles, even where there was bone showing, until they were gone.

Finally, she pressed clean doeskin tightly to cover the entire wound before adding layers of leaves and moss to hold the whole thing in place. The adults helped tie sinew around the Summer Swan's body to make sure it all stayed tight. Only then did Speckled Fawn rise to leave. For the first time, they were aware of the babies nearby, crying for the breasts that fed them. She left hurriedly and soon the air was quiet as the babies found their food.

Inside the tepee, Little Crane carefully covered the prone woman. She announced, "I am staying with her tonight and father can stay, too. Uncle, the terrible twins need you. If there is any change, I promise to call you." No one questioned the girl giving orders to her grown family; they simply obeyed.

Chapter 35

The call they hoped to hear did not come that night, the next, or the next. Summer Swan did not awaken or move in any way. Several women came to take turns turning her, cleaning her, and dribbling water between her lips.

Sweet Flower, leaning on Little Crane, came each morning and afternoon to rub buffalo oil all over the woman's body, mostly on her arms and legs. She would bend them at all the joints as Summer Swan had done when she nursed the nearly dead Sweet Flower. She showed the others what to do and left them the chore when she returned to the many children who slept in her tepee. It was not long until care for their special woman was part of the routine of tribe members. At night, the two men who loved her took turns holding her and begging the gods to give her back to them.

Summer Swan knew nothing of this, as she lived now in a world that only she could know. Her first memory was of her mother and father playing with her before her bedtime. She did not know how old she was, only that it as the happiest time of her life. She loved her parents and knew they loved her, too.

Sometimes her memories stayed for long periods, but mostly they dissolved quickly, leaving her sad. She thought they were dreams, but could memories be dreams? She followed her mother everywhere, learning what all Indian women learned. Even as a child, it was apparent that she was special. She seemed to have insight into what roots and herbs to pick, what tree bark healed burns, and the kinds of lizards and small creatures that could help the ill. Her mother explained that it was a gift from the gods handed down from mother to child over the ages with each generation more gifted than the previous.

In her unconscious world, Summer Swan felt fright, as she knew what was next. She did not know how she knew, but she did and it was horrible. The hunters were chasing a large herd of buffalo, bringing down many for their winter supply. No one ever knew why it happened, but the herd suddenly turned and stampeded back on the hunters. There was no escape for the four trapped in the running ocean of giant beasts and their sharp hooves. One of them was Summer Swan's father.

Had anyone been watching her at that moment, they would have seen her body give a startled jump and tears on her cheeks. All was still again.

* * * *

Summer Swan's inert body lacked nourishment and began to thin. Speckled Fawn boiled some deer meat and fed her the broth. Next time, she added vegetable. They gave her as much as she would take, which was little, but it was enough to slow the weight loss. However, with the soup came the need to change her diapers more often, a task no one liked to do. Even her men found excuses to avoid the task. Little Crane and Speckled Fawn were the only members of the tribe to do the job. One afternoon, Speckled Fawn was sure she heard a sound from the pale lips, but only once, so she mentioned it to no one.

Summer Swan, as the child she had been was running down a hill with her mother. They had been seeking wild vegetables when a group of unfriendly warriors suddenly surrounded them. They shouted for help, but the wind blew in the wrong direction. No one heard them.

One warrior laughed as he scooped her up. She struggled until he tired of it and hit her so hard she saw nothing for a time. When she finally lifted her head, she was on the ground. She tried to sit up, but a strong arm lifted her again. As she turned, she saw her beautiful mother under a man while the others laughed and waited for their turn. Summer Swan tried to escape the arms holding her, but they were too strong. She watched helplessly as her mother was used twice more before one of the men tied her to the back of a horse. The child did not know if her mother was dead or alive, but decided she must be alive or they would have left her for the buzzards.

No one harmed Summer Swan. The next day they arrived in a village of their own. One of the men pulled the child from her horse and shoved her toward a large fat woman who laughed and grabbed her arm. She could not understand all of what they said, but enough to know she was to work and do whatever the fat woman told her.

Her mother was unconscious and placed in a tepee with another fat woman who began to bring her back to life, slowly. The tribe members wanted them both well and healthy as Summer Swan was now a slave and her mother was bargaining power for passing tribes in need of an adult slave or just women for their beds.

They would not let her see her mother and she suffered several beatings for trying. The third beating was severe enough to keep her abed for two days. Only later did she learn that during those two days, their captors took her mother away to use and sell. She never stopped loving her mother and forced herself to think only good thoughts. Thoughts like she had escaped and was searching still for her daughter. Summer Swan vowed she would never stop looking for her mother, either.

Chapter 36

Summer Swan grew from a small child to a big girl old enough for her first moon, but the fat old lady who kept her did not want anyone to see her as she was for fear of losing her slave. The old woman cut off Summer Swan's hair and forced her to wear tight clothes around her chest to flatten her budding breasts. The old woman kept the girl with her at all times.

One day she sniffed the air, then moved closer to Summer Swan. "Girl, you stink. When is the last time you washed?" Well, never mind. Today you go to the river and wash your body. Take a water bag with you so anyone who notices will think you are going for water. I would go with you, but I am too tired."

Ha, too fat, thought Summer Swan, for such a long walk.

"You be back here before sunset or I will switch you until your legs bleed. Go now."

Summer Swan was delighted most of a day by herself, and water in which to clean. She ran across the plain, knowing that no one would pay any attention to her because her owner was so harsh and she must hurry. She reached the river and waded in without removing her clothes. It felt wonderful. As she floated, an idea formed in her mind. She filled the water bag and leaned it against a tree. She took off her wet clothes and hung them over rocks to dry. She moved away from the river and into the trees and shrubs that lined the banks. It took some time, but eventually, she found what she sought. It was a high cave, nearly hidden by the treetops. It was perfect!

Later, back in the tepee with the snoring fat woman, Summer Swan quietly gathered things she might need and ones the woman would never miss. She took several water bags, three knives of difference sizes, some pottery from which to eat, and an assortment of cooking pots and bowls made from buffalo stomachs. She hid them under her sleeping robes, sure the women would never look there. When it was safe, she would move the items a few at a time to hide under a hollow log surrounded by grass not far from the village, but far enough no one would notice.

She made it a point to cause herself to smell bad by rubbing rotten food and dog dung on her legs every few mornings so the women would send her away to bathe and bring water. She pushed wild onions in her nostrils so she could not smell herself, and their odor only enhanced her foulness. On each trip, she took a few things from her hidden cache. Her routine became the same each time: bathe, wash clothes, fill water jug, climb to cave, hide her possessions. She could smell a creature that lived there in the past, maybe using it even now on occasion. She would face that problem later.

Weeks passed and men were beginning to take note of her developing curves. She knew time was getting short, so each night she would hide larger and heavier items to take. The nights became shorter so she waited until the old woman was asleep before she ran off to the river where she hid these things. Buffalo robes, a bow and many arrows, as many clothes as she could steal, food supplies, and a tomahawk all went to the cave.

The night she left for the last time, she wore the old woman's heavy winter cloak. It was too big, but she could cut it down to fit and have enough left over for a real dress. It started to snow when she neared the river. Ha, no tracks for them to follow, she thought.

The next morning, high on the side of the hill, she could see for miles in every direction. Off in the distance near the village, she could see figures on horseback. She knew they were searching for her, but without any enthusiasm. It was, she knew, because she was of no real value to them and besides, no one liked the mean old fat woman.

Her world became calm and she felt the first sense of freedom in her life. No one bothered her, no one shouted at her, no one hit her, and no one owned her. During the moons that followed, she matured into a woman, learned to shoot her bow and arrow with enough accuracy she could stop a rabbit or a snake from a fair distance. She did not kill larger animals, although she could, because she had no way to smoke the meat, tan the hides, and other necessities.

Summer Swan liked to practice with her weapons, but the tomahawk was the hardest to master. Time and again, she would miss her target, sometimes so far off she had to laugh. Retrieving the weapon after a throw one afternoon, in a pique of anger she tossed it back toward her cave. She slapped herself in the head for not thinking of that before. She set up two targets, so all she had to do was walk to where the tomahawk lay after missing the first target and throw it back at the other target. This proved to be valuable, too, because she had to learn to throw it from different terrain, from different levels, and toward an assortment of different types of targets. Her aim improved, but not to her satisfaction.

Her cooking and warming fires were deep within her cave. The direction of the wind determined when or if she could use them, for she feared her smoke might alert someone to her location. Those times, she ate small amounts from her supply or from her recent kills. She did not go hungry.

The days grew shorter and the nights longer. She loved the freedom to walk along the river or into the prairie and even climbed a tree now and then. She never felt lonely as long as she could hear the birds sing, the small creatures scurry around, and the large ones howl at the moon.

The sound from the cave's entrance brought her to a sitting position in her sleeping robes. She had no fire this night because the sky was so clear that she could see for miles, thus someone else might see her. A figure moved inside, silhouetted against the bright moonlit sky with a million stars. She smelled it and fear took over her body and froze her mind. A bear! And it had smelled her at the same time, giving a loud growl as it ran toward her. Not until later would she remember what happened then. Her instinct to live rose just as the beast lifted itself up on it high legs, ready to attack. It's gigantic mouth opened and one huge paw swept down to scrape her butt as she flung herself out of its path. That angered the creature, which turned to follow her movements. As she rolled, her hand encountered the tomahawk. He stood again, opened his mouth and the tomahawk, aimed at its chest, and entered the cavern in its head embedded itself in the skull, penetrating the brain. For once, her missed target saved her life.

She sat where she was, bow and arrow ready, in case the bear moved again. It did not, but she was too weak with fear to move either. She pulled her sleeping robe around her and crept to the cave opening, staying as far away from the smelly mound on the floor. She ran outside and climbed the nearest strong tree without thought that bears can also climb. Summer Swan had never been so scared, ever before.

For the first time, she really understood the dangers of her freedom. She cried softly and watched the moon make its way across the incredible sky. She prayed to the gods for protection. She thought of praying to her mother, but to do so would admit she thought her mother was dead, and she could not accept that idea.

She did not return to the cave until the sun was well above the hills to the east. It was not an enormous bear as she thought in the night, but rather an average sized one. It was too heavy for her to drag too much for her to eat. She had no idea what to do with it, although she realized that it would rot and her cave would be inhabitable.

Then something worse than the bear happened. She saw a group of warriors coming up the side hill toward her. She ran into the cave to hide, but one of them saw her movement. They began to follow her, laughing as they did so. She understood one of them to say instead of the bear they were hunting, they found a different piece of meat, one for their cocks, not their stomachs.

She found her knife just as one of the men reached her. She brought it up from her side into his stomach. He screamed and held her by her hair until another arrived. She tried to cut the second man but he was too strong and took the knife away from her. She pushed toward him, trying to reach the knife in an attempt to stab herself, but again he was too quick.

The man on the ground was bleeding from his stomach, his mouth, and his nose. He died within minutes. Summer Swan struggled from her captor who, rather than fight her, simply hit her on the back of her neck.

When she awoke, the man was between her legs, rutting like an old hog. This was the first time she was ever raped, but it would not be the last.

Chapter 37

As young as I was, I understood that something dreadful had happened. So much shouting, angry voices, crying women, and a few men as well told me this, but it was not until I realized I had not seen Summer Swan for several days. I did not see them bring her to her home, as it was very dark by then. I made a point of watching closely and listening carefully, although it was hard when the winds blew their words away from me. Whatever the problem was, I knew she was still alive. No body had gone to the burial platforms for a long time. It was a dismal time, I could tell, because there was so little laughter. I wish I knew what was wrong. Maybe this little tree could help.

In her tepee, Summer Swan eyes were moving behind the lids. Big Bull said she was dreaming and that was good. He came to rub her legs and arms with oils and even changed her clothes, noting that she was pale and too thin. He sat for hours beside her in the dark tepee, praying to the gods for some sign and begging them to spare her. Each day that passed lessened his hope that she would regain consciousness.

Behind those eyelids, Summer Swan remembered the long nights when the warriors who captured her took turns with her body. They were careful, for whatever reason, not to hurt her. Probably because a dead body could not satisfy their needs. However, as the months passed, she grew thinner and gaunt until their desire for her diminished to the point they no longer wanted her. They wandered near a strong village, one they knew better than to try to raid, and offered her to anyone who wanted her. Finally one man offered them a water bag of something alcohol, and they accepted it.

The man was nice to her, as were his other two wives, at first. She helped with the chores, which pleased them all. On a good diet, she began to gain weight again and the luster returned to her hair. The sparkle of her eyes and the color of her cheeks gave her a strange beauty that everyone in the tribe began to notice. Two men approached her master to buy her, but he said no. One night, he took her hand and drew her to his sleeping robes, where he made tender love to her. She did not respond at first, but he was patient and soon aroused her enough to feel her juices flow. Soon she moved under his fingers, then his penis, until she climaxed.

He announced the next morning that he would wed her, which he did that very day. His other wives turned on her like a pair of hungry wolves, hitting her and abusing her whenever they could out of his sight. Summer Swan held her words. Instead of complaining to him, she used her body to inveigh herself to him in every way he wanted. He no longer bothered to bed his other wives, but looked forward to every night with her. She had missed two-moon cycles before he noticed and was delighted that she carried his child. His other wives never conceived, which increased their hatred of her, even so far as to question his paternity. He banished them both from their home for two nights, telling them to return only when they sweetened their tempers.

His death less than a moon before her child was born gave her a fear of the unknown ahead. She could not stay here, but where to go? That unknown changed when Soaring Eagle came upon her as she gave birth under the trees.

* * * *

"Now, listen to me," spoke Little Crane in a low voice before entering where Summer Swan lay unconscious. "You can only go see her if you stay quiet. As quiet as a mouse, do you understand?"

"Me hear mouse make noise," said Iron Eyes.

"Me hear mouse talk," said Land Hunter.

"Well, maybe you did, but you will be completely quiet. If you do not, I will take you back home and take a stick to your butts." She lifted the flap and entered with one little boy on each side of her. She knelt by the bed as the twins stared with sad eyes at the woman they loved.

In a whisper that would wake the dead, Iron Eyes asked. "When will Summer Swan wake up? I miss her."

"Me too," mimicked his brother who jumped back as if bitten.

He pointed and all three children looked into Summer Swan's brown pools above a smile. "Hello, my children. I am back. Now come and give me hugs."

Chapter 38

The noise that exploded from Summer Swan's tepee was enough to bring the entire village on the run to see what happened. First through the flap was Speckled Fawn who was planning the wash her patient. She stopped dead still trying to take in the site of Summer Swan sitting up with three laughing, crying, and beyond excited children all over her. Little Crane sat beside her, arms around the woman, crying softly as she planted kisses everywhere she could find to put them. Two wild-eyed little boys bounced all over the bed and the woman, demanding endless hugs.

Summer Swan's laughter rolled through the open flap to the astonished ears of those close enough to hear and that included her two men. They pushed the others aside in their frantic race to enter, and when they did, their reaction was the same as Speckled Fawn. They stood in euphoric disbelief.

I cannot tell you exactly what happened, but I do know that that evening the tribe had the biggest celebration I have ever seen in their village. Even from my distance away, I could hear the laughter, shouts, and merriment that went on until daylight. Soaring Eagle carried Summer Swan from her tepee and sat her on a high log where she could see all that happened and all could see her. She held first one of Speckled Fawn's nursing babies, then the other, snuggling them like kittens against her cheeks. Her flat stomach told her she was not pregnant anymore, but being alive seemed enough for her this night. As the day turned to night, the revelry quieted but continued well into the night. The last I saw Summer Swan that night was in the arms of Tall Tree with Soaring Eagle walking beside them as they disappeared into her tepee.

Holding her in his arms was like holding the brightest star in the sky to Tall Tree. He gently pressed his lips to hers savoring her taste as Soaring Eagle lifted her hair to plant soft kisses on her neck and cheeks. The kiss with Tall Tree ended, and so turned her head to kiss her other man. She sighed deeply.

"Please sit me on my bed, on the edge, between the two of you. I want to feel you both. I want your kisses and embraces. I cannot yet give you my body, but I can give you my heart, arms, and mouth. I want to taste your skin and feel your strength. I do not know how long I was gone, but it feels like an eternity."

"It has been as many eternities for me as there are stars in the sky," said Soaring Eagle, as he took her face in his hands and kissed her gently on the lips. She responded with her tongue that sent a bolt of lightning through his body. She moved her face toward Tall Tree and offered her lips to him.

"You taste like nectar that only the gods can make, beautiful woman," whispered Tall Tree as he licked her lips. Her tongue darted inside his mouth the taste him, sending a bolt through him as well.

"I am very tired and need to sleep. Please, go now back to your children and let me rest. It is hard for me also, because I want to love you, every inch of you, but that must wait. First, I have to grow stronger. It is possible, probably a fact, that I will not walk again, but we must plan to take each day as it comes.

They argued that they should stay. What if she needed something? What if she was got hungry? What if, what if, what if? She put a hand on each pair of lips and shook her head. "Go now, please. I will be fine. And no checking up on me all night, either. And that goes for you too, Little Crane," she yelled, knowing the child was outside waiting for her to sleep before sneaking in.

The warm days of summer began to shorten and cool, with life in the village was wonderful. Everyone wanted to do something for her, so she began to ask for his or her help. "Can I have a long log as high as I sit? That way there will be room for others who want to join me." She got more than she asked for because within the afternoon hours, three long logs arrived and laid out in a loose triangle with ample room for sitting and with space to move in and out between the logs. One sat a bit lower for all for the short legs of the children, and one was higher for the long legs of the men.

She smiled through her tears at their kindness and asked everyone to join her in thanks to the gods for letting her live and for giving her such wonderful friends. She raised her eyes to the sky and chanted. Soon voices joined her and she felt emotions in her mind and body that were new to her. Her eyes closed and she sat stone still for a long time after they quieted.

After a great deal of time had passed, she raised her head and opened her eyes. "Man of Horses spoke to me. He said our lives will be good, but that there will be some things, which will not go our way, and we must be ready to accept them. He did not say what those things might be, only that we must always be on the lookout for snakes and scorpions and thorns and poisons. He did not mean those things themselves, I think, but as omens for which we must watch. Now, I am tired and need to sleep. Goodnight." Before Tall Tree could pick her up, there came the questions she dreaded. "No, Man of Horses did not tell me if I would walk again."

The days passed quickly. It had been a good summer for gathering supplies stores for the winter cold months. The scouts spotted another large herd of buffalo meandering its way toward their camp, giving the hunters one last chance to add to their larders. They departed before dawn, leaving many warriors behind to guard the camp, but taking most of the young men. They needed more experience and what better time than when this herd would give them an abundance of supplies and give the novice hunters a chance to practice their skills?

Big Bull and Summer Swan sat on her log, watching the children at play. "Summer Swan," he asked, "Your men have not been coming to your bed anymore. Why is that? They have needs and they love you."

She sighed. "I am hoping they will find it necessary to seek other women. I do not think I can give them children anymore and they need more sons. Their needs will grow as long as I deny them my body, until they realize they most empty their loins elsewhere."

"You are a young woman who has needs, too, are you not?"

Again, she sighed deeply. "Yes, I suppose I do. I did not think I did until they kissed me and I felt my body respond. I am not a man, though, and can control those needs."

"That is not a good thing, Summer Swan. Do you not think the decision for children should also be theirs? Soaring Eagles has two sons and Tall Tree has Little Crane. She is not male, but through her, his blood will not be lost."

"I will think on it, Big Bull. There is time."

They sat in companionable silence for a long time. Suddenly, Big Bull stood and limped over to where the children played. He spoke to them a long time before he returned to her log. The children scattered in many directions only to return to him, carrying an array of sticks and tree limbs. Even the tiny ones carried sinew. They all sat on the shortest log to watch. Big Bull began by laying out the longest branches until he found four about the same length. Next, he located several in uniform lengths, which he tied matching pairs to the long ones making what looked like thin ladders. He bound the bottoms of each of two pair of them together along with a short sturdy piece. Across the top of each, he tied a wide piece, then stood them up.

"Here, Summer Swan, try these. Put one under each of your arms and hold one of the lower pieces like a handle. Now, carefully, put your weight on the top and lift yourself to your feet, but using the thing for balance."

She did exactly as he said. She stood erect, for the first time in seasons. However, the pressure of the wood under her arms gave too much pain for her to continue. She explained the problem, and finally Little Crane spoke, "Wait, I know." She took off at a dead run and returned quickly. In her hands, she had small pieces of buffalo pelts, soft and pliable. Big Bull took the 'things' back from Summer Swan and bound the pelts to the top, giving a soft surface that was painless when the woman stood once again.

In years to come, I would learn these were called crutches and not a new thing in the world. They were new only to us. I can still remember the shouts of the happy children and men who watched the process of getting her back on her feet. The hunters were returning and heard the shouts. They ran their horses, thinking something was wrong. Soaring Eagle was the first, sliding off his horse before it even slowed. I wish I were closer so I might have seen the look on his face to see his woman standing. Tall Tree did not stop after dismounting, but ran to her, taking her into his arms and holding her so tight, she laughed and asked him to release her.

Summer Swan took no time in learning how to move about on the crutches. Soon she was everywhere, even out in the grassland looking for her roots and vegetables and herbs, always followed by a crowd of children. They were ready to dig what she found and run with it back to the village. Soon, several began to locate them on their own, much to the delight of Summer Swan. As usual, Little Crane never left her side and as Summer Swan tired, the child would insist she rest on a rock or log. The world was good, at least as good as if could be with a crippled Summer Swan.

Summer Swan watched her men every opportunity she found. Neither of them appeared to be the least bit interested in the other woman, except for Speckled Fawn. Together or separately, they made conversation with her every time they encountered her, but even to Summer Swan's hopeful eyes, the men showed no sign that there was any courtship intended.

Her body reacted to every touch or smell of either of them. By the gods, she needed them. She fought her desire until she realized she was punishing not only her men, but herself as well. This day, as the pair mounted their horses for a day of casual hunting, she met them at the edge of the village.

"No, no need to dismount." She looked up at the faces she loved. "I would like to invite you to my bed tonight if you would like. I have missed you both so much."

Her men did not say a word, only nodded. She turned back into the camp, bewildered by their lack of enthusiasm. Little did she know that it was what they had waited to hear for so long, they were speechless. They rode without a word until the village was a dot on the horizon before Tall Tree raised his hand and shouted the loudest sound of delight he could, hoping the gods could hear. Soaring Eagle joined him. Soon they were laughing just like a pair of children and they both felt years younger.

Summer Swan helped around the fire circle, cooking and washing pots. It was just about dark when she left the others to return to her tepee. She stripped herself naked and washed her entire body from the water bags the children brought her that afternoon, a daily occurrence. She rubbed fragrant roots all over her skin, even on her hair. She shook out the sleeping robes and carefully folded the top one, sure they would have no use for it until morning. She lay on her bed and waited.

Sometime in the night, she felt cold and realized she was still alone. The moon was high as it shown down the smoke hole. She covered herself with her robes and lay back wondering what had happened that the men did not come. She remembered that they did not say they were not coming to her but then again, they had not said they were. As the hours passed and the sky finally lightened, she knew the reasons. They were tired of the woman with no legs. They felt no desire for a female who could not have sex like a real woman. Her affliction was abhorrent to them. Oh, yes, they might be friendly and as before, but only in a casual way. She offered them nothing now in her bed, except a pair of big tits and a suckling mouth. That was not enough for any robust man. As her tears ran down her cheeks, she could understand their feelings. It was quite simple: they no longer loved her.

Chapter 39

"Well," she told herself, "even if I have no legs, I have my pride." She dressed herself and using her crutches, went to help the other women with the morning meal. By the time the sun reached the middle of the sky, the men still had not returned, causing much speculation among the villagers, including Summer Swan.

By the time the sun reached the mountaintops, the speculation turned to concern. Then a lookout signaled the impending arrival of five horses when there should have been only two.

Warriors armed themselves and Big Bull ordered the women and children into their homes. Summer Swan and Speckled Fawn sat on the log in front of her home as Summer Swan confided her dismay and humiliation by the failing of the men to come to her in the night. The two women were closer now than sisters or even mothers and daughters. Their bond excluded all others but children.

Big Bull once again ordered them inside and realizing they were not moving, sat beside them, watching the riders as they approached the village. She could see now that it was Soaring Eagle and Tall Tree and some children on the other three horses. Shouts of relief and welcome met them as they walked their horses to stop in front of the tree on the log.

"Where did you get these children?" Big Bull wanted to know.

Tall Tree dismounted and sat on the adult log before answering. "We were following a bear in the hills above the river when we saw a band of horses off in the distance. The wind was right so we heard the sound of children crying. There were no women, so we followed them. As we grew closer, we saw the children were tied. The man each held a child in front of him. It did not take long to realize these renegades had stolen the children from somewhere only the gods could know.

"We waited until they made camp then, as Soaring Eagle did to rescue you, Summer Swan, we took care of them. There were seven of them, so it was no chore at all for us, and we left quite a meal for the buzzards. The problem was the children, as they spoke differently than we do and very afraid of us. So, we had to keep them tied for fear they would run away and we could not find them. They could not last a day on their own.

"At first light the next morning, we put them on the horses and started back. Then a noise from the trees alerted us. The growl of the bear we had been chasing came us before the creature rushed us. The children screamed, the horses ran, and we faced a huge old male with death in his mind. Soaring Eagle raised his bow and arrow and hit him in the throat, but it did not stop him. He reared on his back legs to attack me but the second arrow from Soaring Eagle brought him down. He was not dead yet, still lashing out, but I came up behind him and parted his skull with my tomahawk."

He shook his head and nodded to Soaring Eagle who continued the story. "First, we had to find the children and the horses. Ours came at our whistles and the others followed. Only one child had fallen and hung on the side of the horse where she was tied. I lifted her down and moved her and one other girl to the horses with the oldest boys.

"The children were still afraid of the bear, so they were no help in gutting it or even tying it on the two horses we picked to carry the bear halves. It took forever to get the pieces up and secured to the horses. So, here we are, two bone tired, dirty hunters home from the wilds. Now, what are we to do with these children?"

Summer Swan spoke quietly. "Untie them and set them in front of the horses. I think we can handle it from there." Little Crane sat on one side of her and Speckled Fawn the other. The children stood with eyes as wide as the moon and fear etched in their faces. Summer Swan bent forward and spread her arms in welcome. The smallest boy started to cry, but ran straight into her arms. The others followed and soon all five were snuggled on or between the three females who whispered and petted them.

Sweet Flower, on her own crutches, joined them, along with several other women. They brought food and water that disappeared so fast it was amazing. Little Crane looked at the men with disapproval, hands folded over one another across her chest. "What is that matter with you? Even if you were not hungry or thirsty, did you think that maybe the little ones might be? Sometimes, I wonder how the twins and I survive with fathers like you! Humph."

As they divided the children to give them places to live, it became apparent that three of them were of one family, as were the other two. Sweet Flower took the two with her and Dark Woman took the other three. Her own child had not lived long, and she missed it, as did her sad husband, so she hoped these children might help fill their void.

The hunters led away the horses, including the bear-laden one for processing in the morning. They tied it to a rope and pulled it high in a tree to keep night visitors away from it. Both Tall Tree and Soaring Eagle were in a hurry, but protocol forced them to stay and help, but it did not stop them from glancing at Summer Swan on her log. What they missed the night before weighed heavily on their minds and trigger physical responses they became painful until they forced the thoughts away.

Summer Swan and Speckled Fawn sat together quietly, each holding one of the babies Speckled Fawn nursed. Finally, she spoke. "My dear friend, it appears you had a sleepless night for nothing. If they had not rescued those poor babes, they could never forgive themselves and they know you would not either if you ever found out. They did the only thing they could do. If you were miserable all night, imagine how they felt. Cocks as hard as logs, thinking of you waiting for them and balls drawn inside like thunder eggs." She giggled and Summer Swan joined her.

Her friend took the babies inside as Summer Swan moved toward her own entrance. A hard hand grabbed her upper arm and turned her around. She had not heard Soaring Eagle moved behind her. He lifted her into his arms and set her up on his horse. He mounted behind her and walked the horse toward the river.

* * * *

She started to ask him a question, but he put his fingers over her lips. "You must not talk now. You must listen until I tell you to speak." Normally, she would have reacted like a bear, but he was so serious, she kept quiet. "Summer Swan, I know what you must have thought when we did not come to you last night. Your self-doubts took over and you felt inadequate. I want to end that for the last time. I love you and want to marry you. No, do not speak yet."

He stopped the horse and waited for Tall Tree to join them. They exchanged nods and smiles. Tall Tree brought his horse as close as it could go and took her from Soaring Eagle's arms. Tall Tree spoke softly and firmly. "Summer Swan, I love you and want you for my wife. No, just listen. Big Bull tells me that our legends tell of a strong woman, so clever and spiritual that the gods granted her three husbands. We are only two men and we want to be the husbands of our own strong, clever, spiritual woman. Now you may speak."

"Is that an order? Too speak, I mean? Did you two plan this? To pressure me when I was bewildered and afraid? To trick me into your plan? To get Big Bull to agree to it? I do not know if this is good or bad. However, I do know that I need to think and you both need a bath. It is a warm night, probably the last, and a perfect time for a swim."

They let her change the subject, knowing her well enough that any further pressure could anger her, something they did not want. They wanted her soft and loving, sweet and pliable, giving her love and taking theirs. But, knowing Summer Swan, as they did, they could only hope for the best. That was one of the things about her that intrigued them the most.

Chapter 40

Summer Swan's head whirled countless thoughts. She loved Tall Tree, but not the way she loved Soaring Eagle. He was gentler, kinder, and more amusing than Soaring Eagle who was stern, militant, and somber. Was it fair to either of them to take two husbands? The idea still spun out of control in her mind. She closed her eyes and rested her head on Tall Tree's chest as they rode to the river.

Her memory ran back to the first time each of them had made love with her. Soaring Eagle loved her like a warrior, hard and strong, while Tall Tree gave her his tenderness and patience. Each was perfect in his own way. What woman would give up either man? She smiled and thought, *I am not that woman*. Nevertheless, they need to wait. After all, *I am a woman*!

The moon was a sliver giving just enough of its light to make out shapes of trees, bushes, and such. Soaring Eagle took her from Tall Tree's arms and sat her on a log. The men seemed to ignore her as they stripping off their clothes and waded into the slow moving water. She watched them swim far across where they stood in the shallowness and talked. She knew they talked about her, but had no idea what they planned. She had not indicated that they could share her body this night, although she felt her desire building as their bodies moved back toward her.

"That was wonderful, Summer Swan, only a bit cold at first, then fine. You should try it," said Tall Tree as he found a long log and laid back on it, full length. In the moonlight, his skin seemed to glow, as did Soaring Eagle who dropped on the sandy beach on his stomach.

"How do you expect me to get there since I do not have my other legs?" she asked.

"Oh," said Soaring Eagle, "Well, all you have to do is ask. Would you like to wash as we did?"

"No," she replied, sarcastically. "I only asked because I wanted to hear my own voice."

The men stood and moved to her. Tall Tree lifted her while Soaring Eagle removed her clothes. Tall Tree picked her up and waded into the water until floated freely on her own. He lifted her head and carefully pressed his lips to hers, feeling her softness and compliance as she opened her mouth for him. Soaring Eagle took one tit in each hand, kneading them softly while his thumbs teased her nipples.

Summer Swan felt the breast react and tighten. She did not even notice the water temperature as her want began to rise. The tongue in her mouth sent shivers over her entire body.

"Touch me. Put your hand in me, please." She did not care who did it. She wanted to feel with every inch of her being. Her wetness mingled with the water as Soaring Eagle moved between her legs. Instead of his hand, he lifted her hips and buried her face in her tangle of curls, licking her deeply.

She felt her fever rising. He was slow and careful as he replaced his face with his groin. Tall Tree held her firmly at the shoulders as Soaring Eagle slide his rock hard cock into her. She turned her head and saw Tall Tree's hardness at her face lever. She took it in her hand and moved it to her lips where she teased it with her tongue before taking it inside her sucking mouth.

Soaring Eagle began to move deep inside her. She moaned, trying to lift her hips to meet him. He spoke with passion filled words, "Let me do it. Just feel." He squeezed her ass with one hand, supporting her, while he rubbed her clit with his other. Feel, he said, and feel she did.

Her orgasm was like a river of fire moving up her body. She cried out as he moaned and shot his semen inside her, giving her one more climax that rocked her again.

She returned her mouth to Tall Tree's quivering organ. Gently she ran her tongue around tip, and then raised her head to look at him. "Carry me to the shore so we can do this right." She did not have to suggest it twice. In a fraction of a minute, she was back on land, bent over the cock that was so hard it was painful. She laughed as he moaned while her hands squeezed his balls. He could stand it no longer and pushed her head down. Her mouth enveloped his velvet penis. One hand caressed his balls while the other slid up and down his shaft in rhythm with her moving lips. Summer Swan always felt excitement when she sucked her men. Her pussy was getting wet again even before Tall Tree moaned and shoved his spewing penis as deep in her throat as possible.

She lay back between her men. To her, they were always "her men." Her wetness and her clit wanted more. "It is your fault, Tall Tree, for my getting so wet. Feel me. See?" she asked as two hands met and slid fingers inside her. "Sucking either of you makes me wet and horny. So, who is going to take care of it?"

"Well," said Tall Tree, "since it was my fault, I should probably have to take care of it." He moved to his knees and spread her legs as far apart as he could. "What do you want me to do, my darling wife-to-be?"

"Fuck me. Just fuck me."

"That he cannot do," said Soaring Eagle as he kissed her lips and neck, running his tongue down to her breasts where he teased her nipples and squeezed her orbs, taking her breath away. "We will explain later. Now, relax and let him do with you as he wishes."

Before she could question further, her pussy sent out rays of warmth from the touch of Tall Tree's fingers inside her canal moving them until she instinctively tried to raise her body with her legs, which she could not. Soaring Eagle sensed her frustration and slid one arm under her hips to lift them. Tall Tree felt her pushing against his fingers and moved them away, knowing she was ready. He buried his face in her sex, covering her clit with his mouth. He sucked it, feeling it grow like a tiny penis, which he nibbled with his teeth until her scream of pleasure echoed over the plain.

They rested, but all the time touching and caressing. She turned on her stomach so she could kiss each pair of lips. "I think you need to tell me whatever was the reason Tall Tree could not fuck me? Do you have a disease?"

"No," he laughed. "It is just not my turn."

"What do you mean your turn?" she asked.

Instead of answering, Soaring Eagle asked her, "Have you thought you might catch a child from one of us and not know who gave it to you?"

She shook her head no, feeling sure she could not bear another child, but said nothing.

He continued. "We have. Even if you do not marry us, that is something we must consider. So, we decided that between your moon cycles only one of us can actually have that kind of sex with you, so we will always know, if you catch a baby, who is the father."

Summer Swan did not speak and then asked, "How did you decide who was first? Did you draw straws?"

"No, actually, the twins did the drawing." Tall Tree said. Land Hunter and I lost, but next time it is my turn. And woman, you had better be ready, because I am storing up starting right now."

She laughed. "Well, we shall see about that." She bent her body until she was lying almost on top of him, with her tongue teasing his cock. He was erect and in her mouth even as she smiled up at him. "Soaring Eagle, I have a pussy right down there that could use more fucking, if you are interested."

He needed no further suggestions as he turned her hips to allow him inside her once again wetness. They rocked and moved together as they reached their zenith one more time before washing again and returning to camp. As Tall Tree carried her into her tepee, he said, "You have not said that you will marry us."

"I cannot answer you right now. I need some time, but I do love you both."

Chapter 41

The cold season approached. The temperatures stayed above normal and what snow fell was good. It brought moisture to the soil and roots of all things on the plains. During those weeks, Summer Swan exercised her muscles every day. She knew her torso and upper muscles were stronger than ever, but her legs did not respond as she had hoped.

One particularly beautiful sunny day, the sun made its warmth known for a few hours. It gave everyone in the village an opportunity to spend time outdoors. The children in particular ran like rabbits, helter, skelter, and yon, on little legs but with loud voices. Summer Swan sat on her log watching them when Iron Eyes scurried to her and took her hand. "Come, Sssswan, run with me?"

"I wish I could, little one. Oh, so much I wish I could," she replied. The look of disappointment on his face hurt her, but only lasted a minute.

"Then, ride horse with me?"

She thought about it, and then stood with her other legs. "I do not see any reason I cannot ride with your father or uncle to help us." However, the child could not find either one of them, so he brought Little Crane and Speckled Fawn, neither of which understood what he wanted.

Summer Swan explained, causing Little Crane to whoop and holler so much the other children joined in without any reason other than they could. Some of the older boys wandered over and soon her plan became a reality. The boys built a series of steps from chunks of wood under her direction, so she could climb with her crutches until she reached the level of her horse that Speckled Fawn held for her. Balancing on clutch, she lifted her other leg with one hand and slid it over the horse. She pushed herself away from the crutch and sat upright. She now sat on her horse, as she had for years before the accident.

I watched all the activity with much interest, as I watched over the village at all times. However, when Summer Swan was involved, it was always something unexpected and this was no exception. I had no hope to see her on a horse again, but there she was. And not only that, but she had two little boys holding tight to the horse's mane as they sat in front of her.

At first, she let the horse simply walk around to the enjoyment of the crowd, but soon she increased it to a trot. This gave the twins more reason to shout and giggle. Finally, she stopped the horse to have the boys lifted off to the ground. She moved the horse to the open space behind her tepee and letting out a yell, she pushed her mount into a run. She raced across the snow-covered prairie, laughing as only a freed prisoner would laugh.

She rode as fast as she could until she felt the horse tiring, so slowed to a walk. Summer Swan tried to remember a time she had been so free, but could not. No one or no thing g could suppress this wonderful feeling, she decided. It was a long way back to the village, but she did not care nor worry about the time, as for her now was all that mattered.

The horse indicated a desire to move toward the river, so she gave him his head knowing he was thirsty. As he drank his fill, she heard sounds above her in the hills. She moved him out of sight behind a stretch of bushes and waited, cursing herself for being without a weapon. Then the strangest thing happened: a man leading a small horse of some kind came stumbling down the hillside to the edge of the water.

She could smell him and it was not a pleasant odor. He stunk of blood, rot and body excretions, but he did not wash himself. He filled his water bags and let his horse take its fill before following the river to the east. His head was covered in a strange shaped hat that hid his hair, and he wore trousers unlike any she had seen. His skin was dirty but light colored, much lighter than hers or any of her tribe. As he passed close to her, she could see the little animal carried animal skins, piled high and tied tightly to its round body. The pelts seemed to be where the horrible odor emulated, but the man was just as bad. She watched him until he was barely more than a spot down the canyon before she urged her horse in the direction of home.

Summer Swan heard the thunder before she saw it, far off toward the north. She recognized the sound of a million hooves on the move. They were far away, but the sound of buffalo is ingrained in every Indian from child to the dead. Her excitement prodded her into a speedier return than she had intended, but the buffalo location was important.

While still some distance from home, she saw a group of horses heading her way. She knew her men and others were out to find her before dark. As they pulled up around her, she could see the anger in Soaring Eagle's eyes.

"Before you say anything, I know where the buffalo are and if you scold me, I might just not tell you." Her words brought laughter to relieved faces.

Tall Trees moved to her side. "I promise no scolding if you tell me. I promise."

She pulled him to her and whispered in his ear, then did the same with every other man, except Soaring Eagle. Finally, he could not help but laugh, his anger forgotten in seeing her save and happier than in many seasons.

On the ride home, she described the strange man she had seen by the river. Soaring Eagle spoke, "You will not ride alone again. He might have been dangerous."

She bit her tongue, not wanting to embarrass him in front of the other men. She did say, "Well, he was only as far from me to you as he walked by me, never knowing I was there. Besides, he smelled so bad I thought my mount might run to get away from him." Again, there was much laughter, except from her two men.

They had no doubt that she would be anything but compliant with them in her sleeping robes this night, and they were right. Soaring Eagle carried her into her tepee while Tall Tree took care of her horse. Her stomach growled loudly in response to the wonderful aromas from the cooking fire. She reached for her crutches as two wild eyed little men burst inside, both talking at once, telling their father about their great ride with Summer Swan. She kissed each little head as she swung upright and using her other legs, moved outside to join the others for the meal.

She had to tell of her encounter with the strange man again. The villagers quieted as they thought of what she had seen. Finally, Big Bull spoke. "I have heard of such men. They go into the highest of hills and catch beavers, otters, and whatever they can catch in some sort of strange metal device meant just for trapping them. They kill the creatures, skin them, and leave the meat on the ground for the scavengers. I do not know what they do then, but they always go east when the weather warms and the animals move down again."

One of the scouts announced quietly. "I saw two of them last moon when I was looking for the buffalo herd. They seemed to be going west with two of those strange horses. They did not go into the high mountains, but followed the big river north of here. My opinion is that if you see one creature, there are others around somewhere. We must find out about them and be wary of them until we know what they want and from where they come." The crowd murmured in agreement.

The night turned cold quickly. Summer Swan retreated to her tepee early, fastening the flap securely behind her. She heard the men approaching but ignored their knock. They spoke quietly and left for their own tepees.

It was long before sunrise when she awoke and prepared for the day. She was so quiet that no one heard her movements until she led her horse back to her stairs where she could board his back. She had her weapons with her and tied them to her mount, as she had done countless times before, but when she could walk. It took a bit longer now, but she did it.

She patted her horse and whispered, "Good horse. You hold so still for me. No horse is better than you are. Today you must trust me and I will trust you. The men will try to make me stay here, but we know better. We are going on the hunt, even if they will not let us go with them."

"No, you will not go with us, Summer Swan." Soaring Eagle's voice was cold and hard. "You will stay here with the other women. We have many able young men and old ones, too, to guard the village, but they do not have your abilities to shoot and throw. Besides, hunting is for men. So, no arguing, do you understand? You will remain here."

Summer Swan expected no less. She did not even bother to answer him. He lifted her down and sat her on her log, leading her horse away with him. "Fine," she thought. "If he wants it this way, then he will have me as compliant and obedient as any wife, for now. The one thing he and Tall Tree both forget now that they share my bed is that I am not their wife. As for sharing my bed, well, that is at an end now, too."

Chapter 42

Summer Swan stayed on the log where Soaring Eagle had left her. She hung her head as the hunters left the village, filing in front of her, one at a time. Most nodded to her, but her two men pretended not to see her. "Well, this is fine, you self-appointed gods. I will see you again sooner than you expect," she told herself.

True to her word, she had the children retrieve her horse and weapons, including a second quill full as a precaution against running out. With full water bags and jerky, she mounted her horse and rode after the hunters. From a high rise, she could see the buffalo herd far ahead, calmly grazing, and the hunters nearby the stragglers that had wandered away from the rest.

The hunters were forced to circle to the right, far from the herd, as the wind had changed. Summer Swan took advantage of that time to circle to the left, a far distance from the buffalo to keep her scent away from them. This maneuver placed her near the herd ahead of the men, giving her time to deliver six well-placed arrows in six large old males. Each arrow found its mark as her ability to shoot was always with accuracy.

She knew the hunters focused on the young for their softer meat and skins, but those she killed would provide meat for jerky, sausage, and other dried delicacies. These large beasts' hides would be the next tepees and other necessities. Summer Swan laughed aloud as she turned back to the village, leaving the carcasses for the men to find and return them to camp. She imagined their confusion at the downed animals they did not shoot themselves. Soon, she was sure, her men would figure it out, but that was half the fun of it. So much for hunting not being a woman's job.

The hunt was a great success even before they found the six dead animals at a side of the herd where they did not hunt. The kills were fresh, leaving only one solution. "Who would have done this and not stayed to take them home?" asked one of the younger hunters.

Soaring Eagle and Tall Tree looked at one another and Soaring Eagle answered. "I can think of only one person I know." His friend nodded in agreement before bursting into laughter.

"What is so funny? I see nothing funny about this at all. I told her to stay in the village."

By then, several other hunters understood and joined the laughter. Tall Tree said, "Just because you told her to stay in the village, does that mean she did? Of course not. She might have stayed if you had asked her to stay, or begged her to stay, but to *tell* her left her no choice but to do as she wanted. You should know that by now.

"Besides that, look around here. Do you see any wasted arrows? No, neither do I. She fired six and killed six. Not one of us could do better. We must face it, hunting *is* for some women."

Back in the village, Summer Swan halted her horse, so she could reach her other legs and climb to the ground. She asked the children to return her horse and weapons to where Soaring Eagle had left them that morning. The children thought this was great fun and swore to her that they would not tell.

Only Little Crane demanded more information. "Summer Swan, did you kill a buffalo?" The woman nodded. "Did you kill two buffalo?" The woman nodded again. "Did you kill more than two?" Nod. "How many did you kill and how many arrows did you have to shoot to do it?"

Summer Swan smiled. "I killed six and I shot six times." Little Crane let out a whooping yell. She was always proud of what any woman did, especially her wonderful Summer Swan. "Now, will you help me?" The child grinned ear to ear as she agreed.

"I want to go to my tepee and change into my night clothes and go to bed. If anyone asks, just say I went to bed early. They will ask, I am sure, but that is the truth, and you need say no more. Besides, I am tired. It has been a long time since I rode all day, let alone two days in a row."

Summer Swan heard the hunters' return and the knock on her tepee flap. She mumbled 'go away,' and pretended to sleep. When the footsteps diminished in sound, she sat back up and returned to her stitching a new dress for Little Crane who was almost as tall now as she was.

After dark, Summer Swan slipped outside and tapped on the flap where Speckled Fawn could be heard playing with the babies. Big Bull was still outside with the men by the campfire, so the women felt free to talk. "Speckled Fawn, we talked about this once before, but there are new things involved now and I have an idea. Would you like to marry again? Or should I ask, would you like to marry two men? I love you like a sister and want you to be happy, as I want to be."

Speckled Fawn stared at her as if she was a crazy fox before starting her sweet giggles. "You want me to marry two men? I would rather marry you. Now, what is this all about?"

"Maybe I did not ask you the right way. My men both want to marry me. You know that. They are incredible lovers, far more than any one woman can handle night after night. So, would you like lovers, too, that we could share, as they share me? Does this make sense?"

"No, it does not make sense to me at all," said Speckled Fawn. "They are your men and they love you. Neither one has so much as looked my way, so why would they even want me around?"

Summer Swan realized she had not thought the whole thing through. She pondered while bouncing the little girl that Speckled Fawn was raising. "I think I see what you mean. Well, that is about to change, starting tonight. Get ready for a night you will remember. If you decide later you do not want to do it, just tell me and I will stop it.

Otherwise, well… Oh, I have one more question for you. Do you remember the nights when your husband came home from a hunt? Do you remember how he could not seem to get enough of you, how he fucked you all night?"

Speckled Fawn's face clouded before she replied. "My husband was born with a crooked leg and seldom hunted. It was painful for him to ride, and I think that is why he died during that buffalo hunt. I think he was trying to be the man he wanted to be."

Summer Swan sat the baby back in its basket and hugged her friend. "I am sorry to bring up sad memories. I wanted you to understand the fury of a man's lust after blood flows in a hunt or fight. It is a wonderful thing to feel, either as the hunter or the woman he fucks."

"Well, if it is so special, perhaps I should try it sometime."

"Perfect, because that time is tonight. Little Crane will take the children with her to Sweet Flower's home. You will have no babies to worry about. Take her to Sweet Flower's, then come to my tepee and you will have a night to remember, I promise. I also promise, if you want it to stop, it will. Just tell me."

Speckled Fawn made a bed of sleeping blankets across far wall, away from Summer Swan's robes. They made idle chatter until the knock they expected came gently on the flap. "Yes" was all she said before the two men entered and headed for Summer Swan. "No, wait. Look around yourselves and see what is new tonight. Tonight you will love not only me, but also my friend. Here is where you decide how you want to do it. Do you want us side-by-side, or apart? Do you want to take turns with us or at the same time?"

The men looked confused. "Then I shall decide. Speckled Fawn come here and let them watch you take off your clothes. Are you afraid? Here, I will help you and then you can help me with mine."

As Speckled Fawn pulled off her skirt, Tall Tree reached for her arms and pulled her to him. He gently kissed her cheeks and neck, waiting to see if she offered her mouth. When she did press her lips to his, he moaned and pulled her shirt over her head. He continued to kiss her as his hands moved to cup her breast, still full of milk. He felt the nipples dribble. "Can I?" he asked her. She nodded and felt an excitement like never before.

Soaring Eagle grinned at his friend before turning to Summer Swan. His tongue moved into her mouth, slipping around her tongue in a duel of feeling. He removed his clothes so quickly she laughed, but the laughter turned to moans as his tongue ran around her neck and down over her tits. He nibbled and sucked until she cried out for more.

Tall Tree's cock jabbed Speckled Fawn's stomach as he picked her up and laid her on her bed. "You are beautiful, sweet Speckled Fawn. I want you. I want to love you. I want to be in you. First, let me fuck you before I come into the air. That is how much I want you." She nodded and spread her legs. She was tense, never expecting what was happening. It was so quick, but so exciting at the same time. He was gentle as he slid his hardness into her barely damp pussy. Feeling her dryness, he pulled out and ran his fingers inside her. She jumped as he touched her tiny clit. Instantly, her vagina sent its fluid into all parts of her pussy. He slid in again. This time it was with power and fullness.

"I am sorry, it is time already." Tall Tree exploded into her, but did not roll away as her husband always did. Instead, he took his nearly hard cock in his hand and began to move it around the inside of her cunt. He pressed it hard against her clit and rubbed it back and forth until her body met his movements. He let the cock slip away and used his thumb to move the growing button in a circle. Speckled Fawn had never felt anything like this, even when she rubbed it herself as other women said they did. Her explosion was like a whirlwind pulling her into its center. She cried out into his mouth as he covered her face with his lips. When she dropped back down, he quickly pulled her into his arms and held her close. She was overcome with an emotion that was beyond her feeling for any other man, ever.

Summer Swan held the throbbing cock that Soaring Eagle rubbed against her stomach. She slid her hand up and down the shaft, loving the way the skin felt. She pulled him up until she could take his penis in her mouth and suck it until he moaned. She took it out and wrapped her tits around it, letting him move in the tightness there. She bent her head and tongued the end of it each time it came close enough to her mouth.

Tall Tree, with Speckled Fawn in his arms, watched the other couple. He let his fingers move around her tits, making the nipple harden as she began to understand how having two men could be wonderful.

When Soaring Eagle moved to his knees between her legs, he lifted them to his waist and pushed inside her wetness. Summer Swan began to rock as his hot cock touched her everywhere, sometimes deep, sometimes shallow, but always building her nerves ending until they could take no more. Her head fell backward, her tits rose up, and together the pair came long and hard.

They all remained quiet until their breathing leveled off. Summer Swan smiled at her friend whose face was partially hidden in Tall Tree's neck. "Now, how was that for a beginning, Speckled Fawn?"

"That was a beginning? How can there be more?"

Soaring Eagle stood and lifted Summer Swan in his arms. He laid her beside Speckled Fawn and looked down at the two women. Summer Swan's tits were large and round, while Speckled Fawn's were pear-shaped with nipples pointing for a mouth to suck them. Summer Swan was larger with wider hips and incredible curves. Speckled Fawn was slimmer, almost like a youth but her legs were long and the thatch between them opened slightly to reveal a clit as large as a small cock, inviting males to dip their faces into the curls the minute they saw it.

He reached down to cup both curly junctions. "Summer Swan, yours is sexy. Speckled Fawn, yours offers your womanhood for instant loving. Would anyone object if I had a taste or two of each?"

"I object, my friend," said Tall Tree. "I want to taste, too. So you will just have to take turns with me." That is what they did until the women cried out, first one and then the other, as they came. Hard cocks pressed against cheeks, begging for relief. Speckled Fawn did not know what to do, but quickly figured it out, taking Soaring Eagle into her mouth. Her fear of him diminished as he moved in and out, as he caressed her tits until he came, filling her with his semen that she found tasted good.

It was time for Speckled Fawn to go for her nursing babies, but she did not want to leave and have this wonderful night end. Summer Swan smiled and kissed her friend's cheek. "If I could nurse the babies, I would and you could stay all night in my place. Bring them here, feed them, and stay for another short time of sex. Are you glad you agreed to do this with us?"

After she returned with the children, Summer Swan explained the problem of catching another baby. "Now, only one man can fuck me, actually fuck inside me, until I have another moon cycle, then they can switch. With you here, it can work that way for you, too, if you want. We much know the parentage of our children because there must be no thinning of our bloods and to insure purity of our blood lines."

The women laid next to one another as their men mounted them one last time that night. It was slow and exciting for both couples, especially watching the movements and excitement of the other. As her wetness flowed down between her ass cheeks, Tall Tree moved his fingers to the hole below her vagina and gently inserted the little one until Speckled Fawn cried out. He moved his finger in a circle until he felt her relax. "This is something we want to try on our women sometime."

Speckled Fawn trembled at his words "our women." Did that mean he wanted her? After this night, how could she go back to her lonely bed and her own inadequate fingers?

"Before you two take her and the babies home, I think you should give Speckled Fawn your famous 'good night' treat, Soaring Eagle," said Summer Swan. "Tall Tree, if you want to try it on me again, please do."

Soaring Eagle carried Speckled Fawn back to her blankets. He lay beside her, resting her head on his shoulder. He separated her legs only a bit before turning his hand over to rub moved it along the upper side of her pussy. She enjoyed the touch, but it was nothing special. Suddenly, a tremor ran through her body as he found the tiny place that every woman has, but few men can find. He pressed hard with no movement. Her hips moved to press against his hand that he now began to move ever so slightly as he increased the pressure until her cries grew so loud he covered her mouth with his to quiet them. Never in her lifetime would she be able to describe what she felt. Only another woman, Summer Swan, could understand.

Tears ran down Speckled Fawn's cheeks as Summer Swan wiped them away. Soaring Eagle said nothing, but did kiss her cheek before helping her rise. She was not sure she had the strength to walk, but somehow did. Each man picked up a child to carry to the tepee next to this one. Inside old Big Bull snored the sleep of a contented soul.

Chapter 43

Summer Swan was already asleep in the short time it took for the men to return to her tepee. Soaring Eagle dropped to his knees and began to kiss her until she opened her eyes. "Go away, both of you. I am too tired for any more and want to sleep." She tried to push him away, but he continued his kissing her face before setting his mouth tight over hers.

She felt the first response from her body and wrapped her arms around his back to run her fingernails in circles over his taut muscles. Tall Tree teased her between her thighs, moving them ever so slowly toward the junction above. Without any conscious effort on her part, her hips widened to invite his touches. Soon she was fully awake again and felt her wetness awaiting caresses, which did not come.

"Please, touch me, Tall Tree. Soaring Eagle, bite my nipples." Neither man did as bid, but stood to move away from her. She was so ready by now that she felt desperation to be fucked. "What are you doing? Why are you stopping?"

"It is time, Summer Swan, to learn that we are men and you are a woman. You have led us like dogs on ropes panting after a bitch in heat. You have made all the decisions without so much as a single question whether or not we liked what you decided. Tonight was an example. You, and Speckled Fawn who was your toy to entertain us, chose what we did and we did exactly what you wanted. Did you ever consider that we might want to choose a woman other than you and that it might not be someone you wanted?"

Soaring Eagle barely took a breath before Summer Swan answered. "It did appear to me that you both enjoyed yourselves a great deal. I doubt that you would ever have even thought of expanding our little trio into something much more fun as long as I opened myself to you, giving you what endless men desire. No, this is not about the four of us together, it is about my disobeying the orders of the mighty chief who told me to stay in camp while you hunted. Your pride hurts because you cannot control me like a child. I am a woman, as you said, and more woman than either one of you alone can handle. Maybe more woman than three or four men can handle.

"This is my thanks for giving you another soft body to enjoy, for thinking you would like to spread another set of legs and slide into another pussy, for giving you more sex in one night than any man could hope to have in a lifetime. Well, fear not, my friends. You had better both pursue other women because this is the last time you will have me together or alone. If you are lucky, Tall Tree, sweet Speckled Fawn will accept you because she has loved you since she joined our tribe.

"Soaring Eagle, your sternness and short temper has frightened most of the females in the village, expect Sweet Flower who thinks you are wonderful and has watched you with love as long as I can remember.

"Now, get out of here, both of you. You are no longer welcome in my tepee or my bed. If I have wants again, I will teach many young warriors on how to please women. From this moment to forever, I will marry no man and I will do whatever the gods want of me." She turned her back to them and closed her eyes. Only after they left the tepee did she allow the tears to overflow her burning eyes.

* * * *

"Well, that worked out fine," spoke Tall Tree sarcastically. "She will be so grateful for our love, she will do whatever we want. She cannot continue to run our lives. She is just a woman!" Soaring Eagle did not reply as his friend quoted his own words. "So, now we will watch a stream of young men go in and out of her bed. Will you listen outside for reminders of what we lost? You are my friend and I respect you, but this is one time I wish I had argued with you."

After returning to their own home, they slept out of sexual exhaustion. Tall Tree awoke with the words of Summer Swan's tirade running over and over in his mind. She had been right, to a certain extent, but she was also wrong. He knew he loved her more than he loved any woman alive, but she did control them as Soaring Eagle had said. However, did he care? No, not really, he thought. She had disobeyed her chief and for that they all three would suffer. Soaring Eagle expected everyone to respect his position and everyone did, except that one woman. He decided to talk to Soaring Eagle again.

The two men met at the cooking fire before mounting their horses for the usual morning hunt for small animals to augment their never ending diet of buffalo meat. Soaring Eagle started the conversation by asking, "Do you thinking she was right? That I wanted to punish her for her disobedience?"

Tall Tree said, "I think she was right, yes. Also, that she should have heeded your words, but when as she ever done so? We have talked many times about her and her abilities that set her above all other women in our tribe, and the men, too. We agreed that the gods tell her things we will never know. They teach her to use her medicines to save lives. They tell her of things to come, like the weather. She seems to know when we are in danger and when it is safe, like those wolves. Do these things make her more than just a woman? Do you know any other woman who can do those things? Besides that, have you ever wanted to fuck any woman the way you want her? I know I have not, but if she refuses us, I will have to find another body to lay with me. I am too young to let my cock wither forever, and I would like more children."

* * * *

Summer Swan did not go to the cooking fire until she saw the men leave. She slept badly and not ready to face them yet. She needed to talk to Man of Horses and his gods to find her future. She took a piece of jerky, checked the fires for drying and preserving the buffalo recently killed, then asked the children to retrieve her horse. She carefully mounted it, dropping her crutches where she could easily retrieve them.

She arrived at the burial platforms and remained on her horse, hoping the gods and Man of Horses could hear her. She began to speak to him, telling him everything she had said and done. She closed her eyes and waited, clearing her mind of everything but her memory of the old man's face. She began chanting softly as she looked into his eyes, but quieted when his words came softly to her ears. For a long time, she listened, until the face faded back into her memories. She turned her horse and slowly turned to the village.

She was almost there when she noticed smoke, too much smoke, coming from the tepee shared by Big Bull and Speckled Fawn. She urged her horse into a full run, waving and yelling at the people, who waved and yelled back. They thought she was just racing her horse as she had done before, never considering anything different about it.

Chapter 44

Summer Swan reached the flap of the tepee next to her own, seeing billows of smoke pouring out around the edges. She slid from her horse, never thinking of her useless legs, and crumpled to the ground. The cries of the babies inside reached somewhere deep inside her, forcing her to pull herself up by leaning on the patient horse. With no thought, she began to move to the flap, pulling it aside. She coughed as she breathed the foul air. She followed the thinning cries of the children until she reached them. She picked them up, holding them against her chest as she carried them to safety.

The other smell she recognized and hated. It was the odor of a burning body. She set the children on the ground and rushed back inside. Enough of the smoke had thinned giving her a hazy view of Big Bull as he lay across the warming fire. She pulled his legs toward the flap, dragging him outside. She sank to the ground by his body, oblivious to her burned hands. He was dead, burned beyond recognition.

Several people came running. The smoke from the buffalo fires overwhelmed that of the tepee burning for those away from the tent, which was much of the tribe. Speckled Fawn ran, screaming and crying toward where Summer Swan sat, now holding the children. Speckled Fawn dropped to the ground beside her friend and took her son into her arms, leaving the orphan girl in Summer Swan's arms until another woman took her.

Only then did they see her burned arms, feet, and clothing. Her singed hair smelled of burning feathers. Only Little Crane had the presence of mind to go to Summer Swan's tepee for her medicine bag.

Men came with water bags that they threw over the sides of Summer Swan's home, to save it from spreading embers.

The twins ran as fast as their little legs would let them, reaching Summer Swan. They began hugging her wherever they could reach, causing her much pain, but she said not a word. They needed to know she was all right and she needed to feel their love. They also babbled about seeing her walking, which all ignored until Little Crane finally listened as she applied salve to the burns.

"Stop talking so fast," she said. "Now tell me again what you saw." Out of their jabbing, she repeated what she heard. "Summer Swan ran into the tepee. She carried babies out first. She dragged Big Bull out." She nodded at the corpse, now covered by a buffalo skin, to stop its burning and to hide the ugliness of his death.

The people looked at Summer Swan who sat without speaking. They waited for her to confirm or deny what the boys repeated again and again. Sweet Flower limped to Summer Swan's side and offered her a bowl filled with an herbal mixture she knew would lessen the woman's painful burns. Summer Swan smiled and drank it while Little Crane forced the twins to move to the log where so many of the villagers sat at one time or another, enjoying the company of the dead man or their medicine woman. No one would ever know why he died, except Summer Swan who knew that his heart had stopped and he fell into the fire.

Two warriors lifted her up to her feet and carefully guided her to her sleeping robes, carrying her, because of her badly burned feet. Sweet Flower and Little Crane helped her remove her burnt clothing, again applying salves. The two exchanged glances that spoke volumes, the skin on the bottom of her feet were black crusts from walking on the fallen buffalo skins that still burned on the ground as she rescued the children and the body of the old man. Could the gods be so cruel to let her walk, only to take that away minutes later by charring her feet?

Yes, they were so cruel, but kind enough to allow Summer Swan to sleep with the help of Sweet Flowers medication. "Little Crane, we must find more of this root and a lot of it, too. Her pain will be unbearable when she awakens, so we must keep that from happening. Peyote, too, if we can find it, will make her drunk as it does the men, also easing her pain, but also giving her visions. We must ask Soaring Eagle to send men south into the deserts to bring it back, because that cactus does not grow here."

"We can put her feet in rags soaked in buffalo oil," said Little Crane. "That is what she did to me one time when I stepped on a burning log." This they did. They dribbled more of the root tea between her lips. "I will go now, Sweet Flower, to hunt for more herbs. I will bring back anything I can find. I will take the other children with me and they can help me find what we need."

She and a dozen older children, followed by a pair of little boys, spread out onto the prairie. She ran from one to another when called to identify something that might be worth saving. This scene greeted the hunters as they drew close to the village.

They raced toward the children. Tall Tree picked his daughter out of the crowd and dropped to the ground from his horse beside her. "What are you doing, Little Crane?"

"Oh, father, something horrible happened. Big Bull fell in his fire and the tepee caught fire. Summer Swan ran in, got the babies out first, and then dragged his body out. Her feet are burned black like a smoldering log drying a buffalo skin. It is ugly and smells worse."

Soaring Eagle rode up with his sons in front of him. "I have been trying to figure out what they are telling me, but it makes no sense. They are saying something about Summer Swan running."

Little Crane repeated her story, crying this time, in her father's arms. She ended her narrative with "Sweet Flower says you must send some men south to the deserts to find Peyote because Summer Swan's pain will drive her mad even if she does not get rot in her wounds."

Soaring Eagle set his sons back on the ground, and Little Crane returned to the others to continue their search. Both men raced their horses as fast as they could run to the tepee where Summer Swan lay drugged.

Chapter 45

The crowd outside parted silently as the hunters entered. Even before they lifted the flap, they smelled the odor of burnt flesh. Sweet Flower looked up at them from where she brushed the singed hair from Summer Swan's forehead. Speckled Fawn sat on nearby with the two babies asleep at her side. She did not meet their gaze, somehow afraid she was the cause of it all because of the night before, but she would not leave the side of this woman she loved.

Tall Tree closed down the emotions he felt. To let them go would create a fury that would lead to killing, himself or someone else. Instead, he dropped to the ground beside Speckled Fawn and took her hand. They sat motionless that way until the babes cried for food hours later.

Soaring Eagle took everything in with a single glance. His eyes filled with tears as he knelt beside Sweet Flower who sat at the side of the comatose woman. He bent to kiss Summer Swan's closed eyes and lips. The pain welled up like a flood inside him. He bowed his head and cried in an anguish that sounded non-human. Sweet Flower pulled his head to her breast and held him as she would a child. He clung to her in the same manner, soaking her clothes with his tears.

"I did this," Soaring Eagle said when he finally raised his head. "I let my desire to punish her for ignoring my order overwhelm my common sense and that is the cause of her condition." He tried to rise, but Sweet Flower held him back.

"No one caused this. Listen to me, Soaring Eagle." She explained for both men exactly as things happened as best anyone knew. "Summer Swan was not thinking of either one of you when she found the strength to walk, then to run, to save the children. She should not have gone back for Big Bull, but she did. She did not know he was already dead and she would not let him die if she could help it. That is our Summer Swan. Now, you need to find peyote for her."

Instead of sending men in search of the cactus, Soaring Eagle and Tall Tree left the village within minutes, not to return for five times of the sun. They carried not only bags of the drug, but also two live plants each in skins hung from the sides of their horses, which they directed the children to plant in containers which could be moved inside if need be.

Summer Swan regained consciousness twice before Sweet Flower dosed her again to make her sleep again. She told the returned men, "I do not like to do this. I do not know how much to give her or how long she can take it. It might be too much. I might even kill her."

Soaring Eagle nodded his understanding. "We have talked about that and decided she should die before having to suffer so much pain. We did talk to a medicine man in a desert tribe who gave us advice on how to use the peyote to help her, but warned us again of the dreams visions she might see. We decided on the way home that she already has visions, so maybe it would be a good thing. We will discuss it at our council tonight and all can speak."

He sat beside Sweet Flower again, comfortable with her presence. He could see many of the burns were better, some already healed over, but those on her feet remained the same. A few days later, an excited Sweet Flower knocked on his tepee flap in the night to tell him there was finally some improvement. He took her hand and led her to his sleeping robe where he kissed her soft lips and felt her response. In his heart, he knew if Summer Swan lived, she would never bed with him again, as she threatened, and that she would be glad for him and Sweet Flower.

Sweet Flower had been with a man only twice before, so she was nearly virginal, but eager. He gently caressed her as he removed her clothes and explored her body until she was breathless and moaning quietly under him. Her tightness was so exciting to him that he had trouble holding back until she cried out. They exploded together, her breathing jagged and deep.

"Did I hurt you, Sweet Flower?"

"No, it was wonderful. I did not know it could be so … so …" He kissed her again, placing her hand on his sticky cock and moving it up and down until she understood what he wanted. He moved his fingers into her pussy, teasing her clit until she begged him for more. Their first joining was good, but the ones later were even better. Soaring Eagle did not find the wild excitement with Sweet Flower as he had with Summer Swan, but he found her calmness and loving acquiescence a pleasure. That special place inside her womanhood he left untouched. It had been for She Who Smiles and Summer Swan, but somehow not for Sweet Flower.

In the darkest time of night, Soaring Eagle crept out of his tepee and quietly entered Summer Swan's home. Speckled Fawn was asleep on a robe near her friend. In the glow of the firelight, he could see the face of the woman who would be is true lover forever. He touched her cheek and sat beside her, kissing her gently. When he looked at her face again, her eyes were open. She did not speak, but moved her lips slightly under his before her eyes closed again.

He suddenly felt guilt at his fucking of Sweet Flower when Summer Swan lay here, in pain, even dying, before remembering her angry words when last she spoke to him. It had been Summer Swan who suggested their mating. Perhaps it was permission as well. He fell asleep with his head next to hers.

The babies crying woke him. He watched Speckled Fawn put one to each of her swollen tits. It reminded him of Summer Swan and the butting heads of his twins as they drained her milk into their greedy little mouths. He shook away the picture, nodded to the woman, and moved to unwrap the burned feet. Seeing them was worse than seeing almost anything else in his life, even the death of She Who Smiles.

The cracked, blackened skin had fallen away, taking with it layers of her feet. They looked as small as those of little children, only red and wrinkled as if they had been in water for moons. There were pockets of infection that even he knew must be burned away to keep them from spreading until they killed her. At that moment, he decided he must be the one to burn them. He had been the cause of so much of her pain in the past; he must be the only one to cause her pain in the future.

He told Speckled Fawn of his plan. She cried but agreed to help. She left to locate Tall Tree who entered with her and Sweet Flower as well. Sweet Flower looked timid and wept softly. He rose and enveloped her in his arms, kissing away her tears. He then explained once again his plan and they agreed to do it this morning.

Chapter 46

They prepared a bed for Summer Swan outside where the light was best to see her feet and gently moved her onto it. The children brought wood and a fire soon flared near her, close enough for Soaring Eagle to reach it as he sat on his haunches at her feet. He ordered dried peyote boiled and cooled enough for her to swallow as Sweet Flower poured it into her mouth, forcing her lips closed so she swallowed. He ordered the villagers away and had robes hung around to protect her from watchers.

All was ready. Tall Tree sat on his knees with his hands on Summer Swan's shoulders to hold her down should she move in her unconsciousness. Her two women friends held her hands for the same reason. Soaring Eagle heated his sharpened knife blade in the fire until he felt its warmth in his hand. His hand was steady as he beseeched the gods above for help. The first cut into the ghastly flesh brought a cry of agony from her lips, followed by a sagging of her body indicating she no longer felt anything. He worked as quickly as he could, making sure he cut out every last sign of the green before he dropped his knife and pressed soft pieces of peyote into each wound before letting Speckled Fawn wrap them again. He moved away into the prairie where he bent and vomited until his chest and throat contracted in pain.

They carried Summer Swan, still on her robes, to a shady spot under an evergreen tree and wrapped her tightly against the chilly wind. Little Crane had insisted on this, reminding them that Summer Swan often took her patients outside, saying the clean air was good for them. Each day, she forced her father and uncle to move Summer

Swan back outside and return her to her tepee during the nights. The child moved her own sleeping blankets to the invalid's tepee and stayed near her day and night. Each day she helped Sweet Flower remove the bandages and replace the peyote when it shriveled into uselessness.

Tall Tree looked down at the face he loved as he sat with his daughter one evening. "Little Crane, there is something I need to ask you." The young woman, no longer a child, nodded. "Summer Swan banished me from her life forever, your uncle and I both. I am not a young man any longer, but I would still like to have more children. Would you care if I took a wife?"

"I would care if you took a wife unless it is Speckled Fawn. Summer Swan picked her for you and Sweet Flower for uncle a long time ago. Sometimes I wonder if she knew it would all come to this. She does see things we do not, you know."

"Yes, I do know. Yes, I want to marry Speckled Fawn. If you plan to stay here with Summer Swan, I will not need to build another tepee, at least not for now." He arose, and then bent to kiss the lips of the woman who ruled their lives even from wherever she lived now.

Tall Tree found Speckled Fawn helping with the night meal and in front of everyone there, he lifted her head and kissed her lips. She smiled shyly and nodded. He took her hand and led her to his tepee. He heard the laughter and joking but cared not. He tied the flap and they undressed one another with kisses and touches. They teased nipples and genitals until their excitement grew to an almost savage joining, much like the first time in Summer Swan's tent some time past. They did not think of that past time, only of the present and the future as they enjoyed each other all through the night.

* * * *

Summer Swan drifted in and out of consciousness, but never spoke. She knew much of what was happening around her and enjoyed her times outside where she could hear the voices of the villagers, especially the children.

Her pain diminished as her burns healed. Her caregivers lessened the amount of peyote she drank and they gave her, which was good. She liked the visions that came to her during those times when the liquid brought them, but her medical knowledge warned her that she might become dependent on it, which she did not want to happen.

This night she clearly understood what Tall Tree and Little Crane had discussed and she smiled inwardly. When he left and Little Crane settled down for the night, Summer Swan softly called out the name of the young woman she so loved. Little Crane was at her side so quickly it as if no time passed. "Summer Swan, oh Summer Swan. Can you hear me?"

The woman nodded and whispered, "Yes, but we must be quiet. This is between us only. No one else must know for a while. Come close, as it is hard for me to talk." Little Crane lay besides her hugging her as close as possible. "I want you to convince your father and uncle that you know the words to marry them, that I taught them to you, and that you will perform the ceremonies. I will teach the words to you and many other things, so that you will be the shaman and medicine woman. From the peyote, a tiny bit, you will learn to have visions as I do until you can hear the gods without it. Each night we will talk until one of your visions tells you it is time to marry the two couples. Now, my sweet child, listen to my words in your sleep and you will learn much."

Each night whispered her knowledge into the ears of the sleeping Little Crane. Every morning, the girl would remember things she had not known before. Her new knowledge both excited and frightened her, but whatever Summer Swan wanted, she would do.

Summer Swan bade her to go onto the prairie and seek a particular root found only after the plant died and that she should dig in the loose rocks under dead tree on the hill. Little Crane was amazed to find she knew exactly what it looked like. "What will I say if asked how I know about it?"

"Ah," whispered Summer Swan, "I have been waiting for you to ask that. You will say that it came to you in a vision, which it did. You saw the vision in the night as I told you about it. My description alone could not have given you the knowledge. The gods gave you a picture in you mind. Go now, someone is coming."

Her visitors were not a surprise. She wondered when they would come, not if they would come. The two men stood above her, looking down at her for a long time. Finally, they sat on their haunches beside her. Tall Tree took her hand and brought it to his lips. "Summer Swan, I wish you could hear me. There are so many things to tell you, but most important is that we have taken your advice and plan to marry Speckled Fawn and Sweet Flower. Little Crane says that you taught her the ceremony. We are here to beg your blessing."

Soaring Eagle bent to kiss her soft lips. "You are in our hearts. Marrying will not make our love for you any less. Tomorrow we will take wives, but you are our wife forever."

Tall Tree jumped up. "I felt her. She squeezed my hand. She understands! Here, take her hand and see if she does it again." The look on Soaring Eagle's face was answer enough. He kissed her again, hoping for some response there but felt none. The hand movement was proof enough to both of them that she heard and approved.

Chapter 47

The sun was bright on the blanket of soft snow that fell the night before. Each bride wore a new deerskin dress she had made and each groom wore shirt and trousers made by his friends for the occasion. Clothes served many purposes, as these became burial shrouds, hopefully many years later. The celebrants never considered that when joining in front of the young woman who wore Summer Swan's special clothing, nor did they think how different this was from the first times they wed when families played important parts in marriages. The deaths in their pasts left no family to participate, so they accepted what Little Crane did and said.

She spoke following instructions exactly as she learned, ending with a special wedding prayer that started the two days of celebration.

Now you will feel no rain,
For each of you will be shelter to the other.
Now you will feel no cold,
For each of you will be warmth to the other.
Now there is no more loneliness,
For each of you will be companion to the other.
Now you are two bodies,
But there is only one life before you.
Go now to your dwelling place
To enter into the days of your togetherness
And may your days be good and long upon the earth.

Summer Swan smiled as she listened to the young woman join her two men to two other women, both women she loved like sisters. She sat upright, legs crossed at the knees, and planned her own resurrection.

She waited until the prairie turned green and her friends were both large with child. Her happiness for them was real. Jealousy was not part of her fiber, but sex was. Her body ached at night for the feel of a man, for the jabbing of a hard cock, for the waves of heat that rolled through her body. It was time for her to rejoin the tribe.

After all, Little Crane had become a woman and needed to be a celebration that time of her life. Summer Swan thought of the young men who would chase Little Crane to their marriage bed and worried the man she chose would be as inadequate as her first husband had been.

She made her first appearance outside on crutches that had been a daily practice in her tepee was the scouts searched for buffalo. She could walk using only 'her second legs,' never putting her feet on the ground. This she did one morning, swinging herself unannounced to the morning breakfast fire as Little Crane walked beside her.

The uproar was loud enough to cause a buffalo stampede, had there been any buffalo nearby. As I know of Summer Swan, I expected something like this. She would never stay forever in her tepee. She was so full of life that she must return to her people, giving them love and care as long as she could.

And that love meant physical love as well as spiritual. She and Little Crane discussed those needs as only a virginal child and an experienced woman could. No question or answer was too personal or when unanswered between the two who were as close as any mother and daughter.

"Summer Swan, I want a man to love me like my father and uncle love you. I want to cry out in the night as their wives do. Oh, I know, we are not supposed to hear them or talk about them or anything, but how can one ignore the joy in them. I am afraid I might never know that joy."

"At one time, we had a plan to make sure that no bride would ever miss that special part of loving. We, I mean your father and uncle and I. Perhaps there is still a way for that to happen. Please ask them, and their wives, to come to my tepee tonight. I would rather you stay away this time. I will explain to you what might happen, but until then, you must wait."

Both of her friends sat beside her on her sleeping robes and she held a hand on each side of her. The men sat on the floor in front of them. Summer Swan took a deep breath and related her conversation with Little Crane to them before explaining the plan she and the two men had devised years ago to teach the young men how to satisfy a woman.

Sweet Flower spoke first. "Oh, by the gods, I could never do that. I love you all, but to let others watch and learn on my body. I am sorry, I cannot do that."

"Sweet Flower, no one expects you to, unless you would like to. Least of all, me. Soaring Eagle either, for that matter. You are his alone and that is as it should be. The same with you, Speckled Fawn. It is your decision alone and Tall Tree would never force you to do so.

"It was a plan that involved only me as the woman teaching the young men. I never tired of your husbands joining with me together, but I know that I can take even more at a time. There is no end, I think, to my need for men. I will not love the young men, only use them to give me pleasure until they learn how to give their wives the pleasure I demand. Do you understand? And you two," she looked at the men, "are you still interested in this arrangement as you were a long time ago?

"I am not young and beautiful anymore and my body is scarred and burned, but the parts that men want all work fine. It will not hurt my feelings if you decided not to participate or if your wives do not want you to. I understand things are not as they were. Only my body inside is the same and I still have those needs.

"Talk about it and let me know your decision soon. There is a particularly good looking young man from our new tribe that shows an interest in me." She laughed and the others joined her.

Much to her surprise, the women joined her outside her tepee early the next morning. They each hugged her and smiled. "We all talked about it last night, both as two couples and separately," said Sweet Flower quietly. "We all agreed that it is something the three of you should do together. Our men love us, we know, but they love you too."

Speckled Fawn giggled. "Tall Tree got hard just talking about it. Thanks to you, I got one great fuck last night. I think maybe at another time, I would like to do it, too, but not until I have a dozen kids first. I remember watching the night we spent together and it was exciting. Could I watch again?"

Summer Swan, Little Crane, and her two friends made boots of white doeskin to cover her feet. At the night fire, Soaring Eagle explained the plan, followed by gasps of surprise and shouts from volunteers. Little Crane smiled as her father selected two young men for the first night. One was her choice as husband. She whispered to Summer Swan, "Teach him everything. I want to scream like you do." Summer Swan smiled and swatted her arm.

If ever a learning class existed like this one, it is beyond my knowledge, but then trees have little opportunity to communicate with one another. I can swear that the noises that came from her tent on the nights that Summer Swan taught were delightful to hear. No one went to bed early except the children. This was too much fun to miss, even for those not participating. Inside the tepee, the scene was designed to drive any man crazy, and satisfy one sexual woman.

Summer Swan wore her white slippers and wrapped herself in a white robe that made her dark skin glow in the soft light of the fire as she sat on her sleeping robes. Both Soaring Eagle and Tall Tree undressed and felt the flame of lust for her that they always had. It was like returning home where only they lived. The two young men were also naked, but sitting across the tepee where they would watch until summoned to join the other three.

Tall Tree moved her robe to expose her swollen breasts. The very thought of what was to come had already excited Summer Swan. Her body reminded her how long it had been since a man touched her. He began by nibbling on her nipples as Soaring Eagle took her face between his hands and kissed her on the eyes, the forehead, the cheeks, and finally her mouth.

The feel of his tongue in her mouth sharpened her senses, making her tongue touch his as she sucked it deep into her throat causing him to moan his pleasure. Her hands moved down his back, caressing the muscles, making her shiver with delight. She cupped his buttock and squeezed. In the distance came a low groan from a man watching as he closed his eyes and imagine his butt was the one being squeezed.

Tall Tree began to lick his way down her body from her hard nipples to her taut stomach. He spread her legs and forced his breath to enter her, something he knew she liked. Her hips moved to meet his as he opened her lips and touched inside her with his tongue.

She cried out into Soaring Eagle's open mouth. He moved his lips to her tits and pushed his throbbing cock into her open mouth. The rhythm of her sucking and hip movement made one to the young men climax into his own hand. The man felt shame but could not stop watching and soon felt himself harden again.

Summer Swan lost track of everything but the hands, cocks, and mouths that worshipped her body. She moaned her climaxes, demanding more. She felt her body rolled over and her knees pushed under her to support her ass into the air. One cock exploded in her mouth as another pushed into her from behind and exploded. Her two men were temporarily done.

Soaring Eagle beckoned the two young men to her side. She smiled up at them as she rolled over onto her back again. "Show me your cocks," she said. "Ah, yes, nice. Would you like me to touch them?" She curled a hand around each, enjoying the smooth hardness and pulsating excitement she felt in the throbbing organs. One was long and thin, the other shorter and fatter. She continued to stroke them until she felt they were close to coming and then she stopped.

"Did you watch the men and what they did to me? Now, you two do the same. Only this time, you will do everything and I will do nothing. I want you to pretend it is your first time with a woman. Let us think of her as your new bride, she is a virgin bride and you must make her feel desires she does not even know she has. Now, show me how you would make love to her."

She pulled the white robe over her body again. "You first," she pointed at the eager one with the long, thin cock. He pulled the robe slowly from her body. He dropped to his knees beside the bed and began to kiss her. He did not know how to kiss until she pushed her tongue into his mouth. She heard is reaction and felt his in her mouth. She teased it, running her tongue around his in circles as she sucked it. "Stop. It is not time for you to come yet. Go on." He pulled away from her mouth reluctantly, but soon became so engrossed in her tits that he forgot his immediate desire to climax.

He teased her nipples with his tongue and teeth and squeezed her tits. He rubbed them against his chest, which she liked and moaned her pleasure. That excited him so much he climaxed on her stomach. When he held hung his head in despair, she took his cock in her hand and moved it to her mouth. He groaned as she suckled him, making his penis move again.

She gently kissed the end of it as she pushed him away. "That was a good start. In a few minutes, you will be ready for your second lesson. Now, you." She motioned to the shorter, thicker rod pointing at her face. He did much the same as the man before him, but he managed to hold off coming until he had kissed his way to down across her stomach.

Tall Tree moved to lie down beside her. He kissed her and rubbed his cock against her body. This time, he moved between her open legs and moved his hands inside her. He spoke, "Inside your woman you must find the small spot where her sex feelings are centered. It is like a tiny rock but if you do it right, it will grow into a small boulder. I think of it as a little penis. It likes teasing just as your own penis does. You will know when you have found it because she will react. Some women like it pinched, some like it rubbed softly, and some like it rubbed hard. Whatever way she likes it, her pussy will tighten and her wetness will flow. It is that wetness that you must make before you try to fuck her. Otherwise, it will be painful for her and she will not want it again.

"The first time you enter her canal, it will be covered with a thin skin that you must break with your cock. Some women find it painful, some not so bad. Either way, if you have done your job of getting her ready, she will forget the pain and focus only on the pleasures. It is a good idea to make her come or close to coming before you push into her. You will know when she is ready. If you are blessed with a woman like this one, her body will guide your way into her. See how she wraps her legs around my back. I know she wants me, as deep inside her as I can go, or around my hips or thighs is fine, too. Oh, by the god, I cannot wait any longer." They others watched as the couple moved together. Summer Swan lifted her hips high to meet him and together they cried out their completion.

Soaring Eagle moved to take Summer Swan in his arms as his friend moved away, exhausted. "She is very tired now. She wants to sleep, but I am not ready for her to leave me yet. See, my cock is hard and wants more of her. I will make her want me again if I can just make her open her legs to me." He nuzzled her neck and licked her tits until she relaxed enough for him to slide a hand inside her dripping pussy. "Now you know how to find her sex button. Here is another way to give her the pleasures she needs. Spread her wide again, and bury you face in her, and find that button with your tongue." He demonstrated until an exhausted Summer Swan began to move under him. She arched to open herself more fully to him and cried out her final climax. He slid his cock into her and rutted like a bull buffalo until he buckled onto her body.

Tall Tree took a cloth and water and began to wash her body. Fluids ran everywhere, both hers and from the four men. He washed himself and offered the water to Soaring Eagle who in turn cleaned himself. "I am not giving it to you young men. I want you to smell the sex on you. We are going to nap a few minutes until Summer Swan is ready to finish your lesson. You will never mention to anyone what we did here tonight. You may want to fuck her again or imagine you love her, but she will never oblige you. Remember what you learned and you will have a happy wife. A happy wife will cry out under you in the night and will bear many more children that an unhappy one."

The young men left the tepee that night having learned to find the little rock and make it a boulder, but not how to suckle it. Summer Swan said that was for them to learn with their wives. They fell in their sleeping robes unable to even think of sex. By morning, they felt it just might be time to take a wife.

Tall Tree and Soaring Eagle returned to their wives and felt desire once again, this time to give pleasure to the women they married. After a night with Summer Swan, it seemed so peaceful to make love to a sweet, docile female. However, to their dying days, sex meant Summer Swan. Love meant Summer Swan. Summer Swan and no other.

The years for these Indians were short, compared to mine. Before their passing, Sweet Flower died in childbirth, as feared. Soaring Eagle grieved for her for many moons before returning to Summer Swan, who refused to the end to marry him. She taught young men the art of sex until her juices dried for all but Soaring Eagle and it was good.

Little Crane married the brave who learned to please her from his night with Summer Swan, which gladdened her, aware that she might have been in a flat marriage but for her loving friend, and she bore him six sons and three daughters.

Tall Tree died in a buffalo hunt in his 40th year. He was an old man by then, still loving two women. Speckled Fawn's children cared for her until she died of loneliness for the man she loved.

Now you know the Legend of Summer Swan. Pass it on to your children and their children. There will never her another like her. As Sweet Flower once told Soaring Eagle, "That is our Summer Swan."

THE END

www.simsbooks.com

ABOUT THE AUTHOR

Beverly grew up on the Oregon Coast where the stormy surf and rugged cliffs make perfect backgrounds for her first novels. Her move to Central Florida, where she lives with her husband, opened a new world of bayous and the critters that live in them, and set the scene for Black Bayou.

They love traveling this great country in their motor home. One such trip became the germ of an idea for an Indian story to be followed by pioneers, ranchers, and all the others in The Witness Tree series.

You never know what might be around the next bend.

To love to write is to love to read.

Siren Publishing, Inc.
www.SirenPublishing.com

Printed in the United States
221700BV00004B/15/P